DANNY ORLIS

AND

JIM MORGAN'S SCHOLARSHIP

&

THE DAVIS TRIPLETS' PROBLEM

DANNY ORLIS

AND
JIM MORGAN'S SCHOLARSHIP

&

THE DAVIS TRIPLETS' PROBLEM

BERNARD PALMER

Danny Orlis and Jim Morgan's Scholarship and *the Davis Triplets' Problem*
© 2024 by Bernard Palmer
All rights reserved. First edition 1968.
Second edition 2024.

Cover image: Adobe Firefly

Character illustrations: John Ball

Editor: Jon D. Fogdall

Aneko Press *Youth*

www.anekopress.com

Aneko Press, Life Sentence Publishing, and our logos are trademarks of
Life Sentence Publishing, Inc.
203 E. Birch Street
P.O. Box 652
Abbotsford, WI 54405

JUVENILE FICTION / Religious / Christian / Action & Adventure
Paperback ISBN: 979-8-88936-042-1
eBook ISBN: 979-8-88936-043-8
10 9 8 7 6 5 4 3 2 1
Available where books are sold

CONTENTS

TOUGH DECISION

The weather in Fairview, Minnesota, was cold and blustery. New snow had been sifting down all morning to coat the dingy drifts of former storms with a fresh white layer. Some of the homeowners had already been out to clear their walks, but many of them had wearied of the endless battle against the winter and were waiting, with some resignation, for it to stop.

Jim Morgan was standing outside the school, shivering as he waited for Connie McCloud. He glanced at his watch again. She had told him she would be out as soon as classes were over for the day. That had been fifteen minutes earlier and still she hadn't shown. He should go on home and phone her, he told himself irritably. But even then, he knew that he wouldn't. He'd keep on waiting for her if it took an hour.

A couple of minutes later she came hurrying down the steps, bundled against the cold, and almost ran into him.

"Hey!" he exclaimed. "Watch where you're going, will you?"

She stopped suddenly.

"I–I'm sorry," she blurted. "I was looking for someone and–" As she spoke, she looked up to see Jim laughing at her embarrassment.

"Jim Morgan! You make me so mad!"

"I make you mad?" he echoed. "What're you talking about, gal? I'm the one who's stood out here for so long I've about turned into an icicle. I was afraid the janitor was going to have to come and chop my feet loose from the sidewalk so I could walk home. I thought I was freezing down."

She wrinkled her nose at him. "That wasn't what I was talking about."

"I didn't think so," he said genially. "Well, come on, let's get on the move so I can get in somewhere and get thawed out."

"I feel sorry for you."

"You sure sound like it."

There was an easy, friendly tone to their banter. The words may have sounded sharp and abrasive, but it was all on the surface. It was plain that their friendship was strong.

They walked up the sidewalk together. After a time Jim turned to her. "I suppose I'd just as well ask you now as later. Would it be all right if I come over tonight, Connie?"

She hesitated.

"Or don't you want me to come?"

"It isn't that at all. You should know that by this time. I'd love to have you come over any time you can, but you know how Daddy is about dating on school nights. He says there's plenty of time for that on weekends."

"I thought probably we could study together."

"I'm going to work on my college application tonight," she told him. "Daddy says I won't get any allowance unless I get it in this week. Some of the kids have applied and already have their acceptances."

The smile left Jim's angular young face. He hesitated to ask what he had to ask.

"Have you decided where you want to go to school?"

She breathed deeply.

"Mother and Daddy talked it over," she said. "They don't like the idea of my going to Bible school."

"They don't?" he echoed. He already knew they felt that way, yet it was different hearing it spelled out so clearly.

"They say that it costs so much to go to college they don't want me to go anywhere except to a school where I'll be able to get all my credits transferred to a secular university in case I want to get my degree from that sort of school."

Jim paused. He felt icy fingers close about his lungs, relentlessly forcing the breath from them.

"A lot of the kids have done well transferring from Cedarton Bible Institute," he said.

"I know." There was no interest in her manner.

"Do you think your dad could be persuaded to change his mind about CBI if I asked Danny to talk with him about it?"

"I mentioned CBI to him, but it wouldn't do any good to have anyone else talk to him. He's got his mind made up. It wouldn't do a bit of good."

Jim tried to hide his feelings.

"Where does he want you to go?"

"There's a Christian college in Wisconsin that has North Central accreditation. He wants me to make an application there."

"Oh."

She stopped and turned to face him.

"You could go there with me if that's where I decide to go, couldn't you, Jim? You don't have to go to CBI, do you?"

"Nobody's said that I've got to go there," he replied, "but that's where Danny, Kay, Ron, and Roxie went. I guess I've always just naturally thought of CBI when I thought about going to college."

She laid a hand on his arm appealingly.

"Why don't we both go to Wisconsin, Jim?" she asked. "It's a Christian school and we could be together."

He hesitated.

"I'd sure like to go to the same school you're going to, but I–"

She misunderstood his hesitation, taking it for interest. "I've been thinking about going to the university instead of Wisconsin, but if you'll go there, I'll go too. Why don't you talk it over with Danny and Kay and see what they've got to say about it?"

"I don't have to talk it over with Danny and Kay or anybody else," he retorted, his voice harsh. "They won't decide where I'm going to school. I'll make up my own mind."

She looked up at him, her lips trembling.

"You don't have to get so mad about it."

"I–I'm sorry."

* * *

On Friday night Jim took Connie to a basketball game. It was a good, hard-fought game that went to three overtimes before Fairview lost by a single point. Kay was already in bed when Jim came home, but Danny was up, still poring over the maps he would be using on the trip he had to make the next day.

"Hi, Danny," Jim said, coming into the kitchen.

"I didn't think you'd be up so late."

"I didn't think I would either, but I've got to work out a flight plan for tomorrow. I'm going over territory I haven't flown over for quite a while."

Jim crossed the floor and sat down at the opposite side of the table.

"How'd the game come out?"

"It was a real chiller, but we got beat 62 to 61 in three overtimes."

Danny whistled.

"That sounds as though it was a good game to watch. I wish we could've been there."

"It was a great game."

He went to the refrigerator and poured himself a glass of milk.

"How about you, Danny? Want something to eat? A glass of milk and a couple of cookies?"

"No, thanks. I've got to get back to these maps."

Jim set the milk on the table and got the cookie jar. For a couple of minutes, he didn't say anything. At last, he returned the milk to the table and spoke. "There's something I'd like to talk to you about."

"Sure thing."

The young pilot leaned back in the chair as relaxed as though he had all night for Jim, if necessary – which, indeed, he had. It didn't make any difference if the boy had a serious problem or just wanted to talk.

"What do you want to talk about?"

Jim cleared his throat. "I'm going to have to make up my mind about where I'm going to school next year and I–I sort of wanted to talk to you about it."

Danny's forehead crinkled curiously. "Yes?"

Jim leaned forward. "What do you think of Clark College in Wisconsin?" he asked. "Or do you know anything about it?"

Danny tugged at the lobe of his ear. "I think Clark is a good school. At least I've never heard anything about it that would make me think otherwise. At least

I don't think there are any Bible-denying teachers at Clark, as they have in some colleges and universities." He stopped significantly. "But I always thought you had your heart set on going to CBI."

The color crept stealthily up into Jim's neck and spread to his cheeks.

"I did think about CBI some," he acknowledged, "but lately I've been wondering about going to some school that's accredited; some school where I can get full credit for all the work I've done, if I decide to transfer somewhere else after a couple of years."

Danny did not answer immediately.

"The important thing is to go where the Lord is leading you, Jim," Danny told him. "If He is leading to a school like Clark, or even a secular university, then He has a specific reason for wanting you there and that's where you should be. But–"

Jim waited.

"But the thing you've got to consider is your motive. Why do you want to go where you do? To me the matter of credits isn't entirely valid."

The boy stiffened. "Why not?"

"In the first place, if you went to a school like CBI I don't think you would be too disappointed in the number of credits you could transfer. Some of my schoolmates were able to do very well."

Jim broke in, his irritation showing. "But if I don't go into full-time Christian service I'd waste a year or more. That's what's buggin' me right now."

Danny's gaze met his. "I guess it depends entirely on how you look at it. I wouldn't say that a year spent studying the Word of God would be wasted."

Jim got to his feet, uncomfortably.

"Well, I–I'll think about what you said," he answered.

Danny smiled reassuringly. "And Kay and I will be praying that you'll make the right decision, Jim."

CHAPTER 2

PROMISING INTERVIEW

Kay Orlis took the opportunity of going to Angle Inlet for a few days to visit Mother and Dad Orlis while Danny was away flying for the mission. Jim could have stayed at home, but Pastor Reeves and his wife invited him to stay with them and he took advantage of it. He didn't think much of staying at home and having to do all his own cooking and dishwashing.

In a generous moment just before they left, he agreed to wash the breakfast dishes for Kay. He had indicated that he would do them that same day as soon as he got out of school. He had planned on doing them then, but he hadn't realized how easy it was to put off washing dishes, especially if they had stood for a while.

Finally, as the time approached for them to come home, he went over to the house, did the dishes, and checked the thermostat to be sure it was all right. When they came in the next day, he didn't want them to find things in a mess. He watched the clock and, half an hour before time for the library to open, he got his coat and headed for the library at school. He had to get a reference book for American history, and if he waited there'd be a line of kids taking turns reading it. And that wouldn't be any good.

He was almost at the school when he paused for a moment. It would be all right to go to the library, but there was a possibility that it had already been checked out. If that were the case, he'd really be out of luck.

Now that he thought of it, he remembered that Connie had said something about having the same book at home. If she did, he could borrow it from her. There wouldn't be any need in taking a chance on getting it from the library. He turned decisively and went to her house. Her mother came to the door.

"Good morning, Jim," she said, smiling cordially.

They liked him, he thought. That was one good thing.

"I'm sorry but Fritz isn't here. He's already gone to school."

Color tinged Jim's cheeks. "Well, I–I–is Connie here?" He knew that the tone of his voice had betrayed the real purpose of his visit.

Jim thanked her and hurried to school. By this time, he wasn't thinking about the reference book for American history anymore. He'd find Connie before class and talk to her. However, before he got to his locker, one of the sophomore boys hurried up to him.

"Hey, Jim."

He turned quickly. "Hi."

"I've been waiting half an hour for you."

"Have you? What's cookin'?"

"Search me." He shrugged his shoulders. "Coach Gardener wants to see you in his office right away."

The lines about Jim's eyes deepened curiously. "He does? What about?"

"Search me. All I know is that he grabbed me as I went by and asked me to wait here until you came in and have you go to his office right away."

Jim hung his coat in his locker and hurried back to Coach Gardener's office at the end of the corridor. Gardener seldom sent for one of the fellows. This had to be something important.

"Good morning, Jim," he said when Jim entered. "I'd like to have you meet an old friend of mine, Gale Hanscomb."

The tall, muscular stranger got to his feet and thrust out a big hand. "Hi, Jim. I've been hearing a lot about you since I got here this morning. Your coach tells me that you're quite a pitcher."

Jim flushed self-consciously. "I pitch a little," he said, "and I do the best I can, but I wouldn't say that I'm that good."

The Fairview baseball coach spoke up.

"Gale is the baseball coach at the university. He was my coach when I played baseball there a few years ago."

"I see."

"He stops by from time to time to see if I've got anyone who might be good enough to do him some good at the university."

"Yes," Mr. Hanscomb continued. "Gardener mentioned a couple of outfielders who show some promise, but my biggest need right now is for pitchers. We're going to be losing our pitchers this year, and there is only one on the freshman squad who gives indication of having the speed and control we're going to need."

Jim stared at him questioningly.

Coach Gardener added. "We've been looking at some of last year's games on film and Gale likes the way you handle yourself on the mound, Jim. He is of the opinion that you may be able to do him some good."

The university baseball coach frowned. "I don't know that I'm prepared to go as far as to say that much on the basis of the pictures you showed me. Let's put it another way, Gardener. The movies show that Jim has a lot of potential as a college pitcher." He turned slightly to address the boy who was standing before him. "If you don't mind, I'd like to see you throw."

"Sure," Jim said. He felt as though he was acting a part. This wasn't happening to him. It was somebody else. He couldn't pitch that well.

But Coach Gardener was talking about him. "Of course, you realize, Gale, that Jim isn't in condition yet. We haven't even started to work out."

"I'm aware of that. I just want to see how he throws."

The coach went to a locker in the corner of his office, took out a catcher's mitt, a glove and baseball.

"We can go down to the gym. There's nobody there at this time of day."

Everything happened so rapidly Jim didn't have time to get frightened until it was all over. Hanscomb put on the catcher's mitt and paced off the approximate distance from the catcher to the pitcher's mound.

"All right, Jim, let's have one."

Before he could throw, his own coach spoke in warning. "Don't throw too hard the first time. Don't take the chance of hurting your arm."

Jim drew back his arm in a semi-windup and fired the ball to Gale Hanscomb. It smacked resoundingly into the catcher's mitt. Without comment Hanscomb tossed it back.

"Let's have another."

Jim threw comparatively slow balls at first until the perspiration began to gleam on his forehead and he felt the muscles in his arm begin to loosen. Then he threw harder. Hanscomb watched him carefully. When he saw that the boy could now throw without risking injury to his arm, he asked him to throw harder and harder. This Jim enjoyed. He went into a full windup and rifled the ball to the baseball coach. Hanscomb nodded approvingly.

"Now, let's see your curve."

Jim nodded and fired a fast-breaking curveball.

"Not bad," Hanscomb said. "Not bad at all."

After half a dozen curve balls, Hanscomb was satisfied. He handed the mitt to his former student.

"I think I've seen enough."

"What'd I tell you?" Coach Gardener asked. "Isn't he university material?"

"You're not bad, Jim. Gardener here has done a good job of teaching you the basic fundamentals of pitching. You've got a good, smooth motion, and a fast ball that's very creditable." They walked back to the coach's office together. "I'm going to leave you some literature, Jim. I'd like to have you look it over and see what you think of the university as a place to continue your education."

The boy did not answer him. He could not. The university coach thought that he might be able to pitch well enough to make the varsity. To be sure, he didn't turn handsprings over Jim's ability or anything like that, but he was impressed. If he hadn't been, he wouldn't have asked him about attending school there at all.

"I'll be back in two or three weeks," the coach went on. "And when I come back, I may have something very attractive to offer you in the way of a scholarship."

Jim's head was spinning when he went back to his classroom.

He glanced at Connie, who smiled shyly and turned away. He wanted to go over and talk with her. He was bursting to tell her what had taken place that morning, how he had been called into Coach Gardener's office and asked to demonstrate his pitching ability to the university coach. But while he was trying to make up his mind whether to do so or not the bell rang and Miss Jamison called them to order and took roll. He was disgusted with himself for his indecision. Now he'd be fortunate if he got to talk with her before noon.

However, as they left the room to go to their second class, Connie fell in step beside him.

"I looked for you in the library before school this morning, Jim," she said, her voice soft and chiding. "But you weren't there. What happened?"

"Something else came up."

She eyed him quizzically. "Like another girl?"

"You know better than that." He was surprised at the forcefulness in his voice. "I don't have time to tell you about it now. How about having lunch with me at noon?"

"I'll be waiting for you at the usual place."

"Good."

The morning dragged by endlessly. Jim took the history test he had planned on studying for in the library before school that morning, but it seemed to him that he had never even heard of half the questions, let alone know the answers to them. All he could think about was baseballs and pitching and the fraternity houses that surrounded the campus. He had heard that those who got into the school on athletic scholarships were really given the rush by the frats. He didn't know whether they got any special consideration in regard to fees and room and board. He wasn't even sure he would want to join one. But he couldn't deny that it made him feel good just to think that they might come and ask him to join.

The next period was study hall and he sat there trying to concentrate and at the same time wishing the minutes away. Connie was considering the university as well as Clark College. If he went there, she would undoubtedly do the same. It might change their entire lives. At last noon came and he rushed down to the corridor just outside the cafeteria. That was the place where most of the fellows met their girlfriends if they were going to eat lunch with them.

Connie was already there.

"Hello, Jim," she said. There was a measure of reticence in her voice. That was one of the things he liked about her. Oh, she let him know that he was someone quite special and all that, but she didn't throw herself at him the way some of the girls did their steadies.

"Hi."

The other kids were forming a line so they could take their turn being served, but Connie stood to one side, waiting for him. As he came up, she stepped forward breathlessly.

"What did you want to tell me?" she asked.

"Nothing much." He was grinning as he spoke.

"But you said it was important. I–I mean I thought you sounded as though it was important when I talked with you."

"I just figured it might not mean much to you. It is sort of important to me." His smile broadened.

"What is it?"

"Well, I've practically been offered a baseball scholarship at the state university."

"No!" Connie gasped.

"That's where Coach Gardener went to school," he explained. "His former baseball coach was here this morning talking to him about this year's seniors. They took me down to the gym and had me pitch for him. Then he told me that I'd be hearing from him in a couple of weeks."

Admiration and pride gleamed in her eyes.

"Oh, Jim, that's wonderful!"

"Of course, I don't know whether I'm going to take it or not," he continued, "but it's good to know that I can have it if I want it."

She stared at him incredulously, as though she could not quite believe what he was saying.

"If you want it?" she echoed. "You aren't serious about not wanting it, are you? An honor like that?"

Jim hesitated. He hadn't seriously considered it, even though it was a great opportunity to get an education without it costing very much.

"Well, I've still been thinking about CBI."

She wrinkled her nose distastefully. "You are?"

"Yeah, I am. I've always figured that I'd go to school there, and I don't know whether I want to change my mind and go to the university or not."

"But they don't even play baseball, do they?" she asked.

He shook his head. "Not that I know of. At least they don't have a regular schedule and play other schools. And I know they won't be giving any free scholarships to baseball players."

By this time, the end of the line had gone away and left them standing there, but they were scarcely aware of it.

"Just wait until Daddy hears about this!" she exclaimed. "He's going to be as thrilled as we are. You don't know it, but Daddy's a great fan of yours. He never misses a game."

Jim frowned. "There's one thing I want to ask you, Connie. Please don't tell anyone about it just yet."

"Why not? I should think you'd want them to know you've got a chance for a scholarship. I would if I were in your place."

"I–I'd just like to make up my mind first."

CHAPTER 3

PRACTICE BEGINS

When Jim got home that evening there was a letter for him from Cedarton Bible Institute. He picked it up thoughtfully and held it in his hand for a moment without opening it.

"I wonder why they're writing to me," he murmured. "I haven't applied to CBI. I haven't even written them for a catalog."

Kay looked up from the evening paper.

"Didn't you want information on CBI?" she asked.

The color faded from his cheeks.

"I–I don't know for sure. I haven't decided yet." He held the envelope up, studying it carefully. "I can't figure out why they would have written to me."

"Danny sent in a little gift last week, Jim," Kay explained. "At the bottom of the letter he asked them to send you a catalog and any other information they thought a prospective student would like to have. That was all right, wasn't it?"

Jim bristled. "He's not figuring on making me go to CBI if I don't want to, is he?"

She folded the paper and laid it aside.

"I'm sure Danny isn't trying to make you do anything you don't want to do," she replied. A question gleamed in her eyes. "But somehow we both figured that you'd want to go to CBI, Jim."

There was a brief silence.

"Well, maybe I will," he retorted. "But I don't want anyone to tell me that I've got to go there. That's all."

Thoughtfully, he opened the letter and read it. He had always planned on going to CBI. He hadn't seriously thought about any other school. But now he wasn't so sure. There wouldn't be any scholarship involved if he did go there. He wouldn't even be able to play baseball. They didn't have a team. The only kind of help he could get financially was an employment bureau. Word was that most of those who wanted work were able to find it.

In a way it didn't even sound as though they wanted a fellow to go to school there. He read the letter through once more and put it aside.

* * *

The next day Coach Gardener stopped Jim in the hall.

"I've been looking all over for you, Jim. How're things going?"

"OK."

"How's the arm?"

A grin lifted one corner of the boy's mouth. "I don't know for sure. It's been so long since I've pitched a game. I don't know if I even remember what it feels like."

"We'll have to take care of that. We're going to start baseball practice next Monday, you know."

Jim's eyes lighted.

"The announcement will be made over the PA system tomorrow afternoon," the coach continued, "but I wanted to talk to you personally to be sure that you'll be out."

"You don't have to worry about that. I'll be there," Jim said.

"Good. I want to be sure you get that arm in shape and keep it that way. If you show the improvement I'm counting on, we'll be building our team around your pitching."

Pride expressed itself in a broad smile on the boy's face.

"I'll do my best."

"I know you will." They walked down the corridor together. At the door to Jim's homeroom the coach spoke once more. "I got a letter from Gale Hanscomb yesterday, Jim. He asked about you."

The boy did not reply, but interest gleamed in his eyes.

"He wanted to know if we'd started practice yet, and he asked how you look this season." Coach Gardener paused and turned toward Jim. "He also wanted to know if you'd decided on the college you want to attend."

Jim hesitated uncertainly.

"I sure would like to play college baseball," he said, "if I thought I'd have a chance."

"That's what I've been trying to tell you. You've got the chance, Jim. Hanscomb is hot on you. If you go to State, you not only will get a scholarship, but you'll also get special attention. He'll see that you get every chance to improve as fast as you can."

The boy swallowed hard. "That sounds great."

"You'd better get your letter off to him right away, then, so he'll know you're coming."

"But I–I haven't made up my mind where I'm going to college yet," he said uncertainly. "I'll have to let you know a little later."

The corners of Gardener's mouth tightened.

"Don't fool around too long. If Hanscomb should be able to line up his quota of good pitchers, you'd be out of luck getting a scholarship with him. In fact, you'd probably have a hard time making the team, even if you did go to school there. So, you'd better get with it."

Jim assured the coach that he would.

He was so excited about starting baseball practice that he could scarcely think of anything else all afternoon. It was still foremost in his mind as he met Connie beside her locker after the last class of the day.

"Guess what?" he exclaimed. "We're starting baseball practice on Monday."

"Oh, that's wonderful, Jim!"

They left the school together. Although it was early in March and the sun was beginning to climb higher in the sky with each passing day, there was still snow on the ground and the temperature hovered around zero. Connie pulled her coat tighter about her throat.

"Have you decided where you're going to school this fall?" she asked.

He shook his head.

"Coach Gardener asked me the same question today. He said he'd gotten another letter from the baseball coach at State asking about me." He glanced in her direction. "Why?"

"Well, Daddy has been insisting that I decide where I'm going so that I can get my application in." There was a short hesitation. "Before I do I–I want to know where you're going."

They crossed the street before he replied. "Coach Gardener says I've got a good chance of being a starting pitcher if I go to State. In fact, he says he thinks I've practically got it made."

Her eyes brightened.

"That should settle it, then, shouldn't it?" she asked.

He shook his head.

"I don't know for sure. Every time I talk with Danny or Kay or Pastor Reeves, they try to give me the old song and dance routine about going to CBI. I get so confused I don't know what I want to do."

Connie frowned petulantly.

"Danny only wants you to go to CBI because he and Kay went there. You shouldn't go to a school that isn't accredited. It's just a waste of time."

Jim spoke quickly.

"I don't know much about credits or things like that," he said, "but CBI's a good school. I know. I've been around there lots of times."

"It's probably all right," she admitted with reluctance. "But you wouldn't be able to transfer your credits to the university after you've gone to CBI."

"Maybe not all of them, but Danny said that it's surprising how many credits are transferable from Bible institutes and Bible colleges. He feels that even if a person didn't get any credit for the work he did at Bible school it would still be worthwhile because it would ground him in his faith."

She thought about that for a moment.

"I suppose that's all right for someone who hasn't been raised in a Christian home and doesn't know much about the Bible, but for someone like you or me, I don't see why it makes any particular difference. We've already had good Bible training."

Jim took a deep breath.

"When I talk with Danny or Pastor Reeves, I get to thinking there isn't any place like Bible school. But when I talk to you or Coach Gardener, I get to thinking it would be better for me to go to State. I don't know what to do."

"Why don't you come over to the house and talk with Daddy one night soon?" Connie suggested. "He's been a Christian for a long while. He could advise you on what he thinks is best."

Jim's forehead crinkled. "I might do that one of these days if I don't make up my mind before then."

"If Daddy will let me, I'm going to wait one more week before I send in my application." Her voice softened. "I'd sort of like to go to the same school you're going to, Jim."

He grinned.

"Now that would suit me just fine."

* * *

Jim planned on going over to see Pastor Reeves that night and talk with him about the various Bible schools and colleges in the area. However, when he stopped by on the way to the library, the minister was at the hospital on a call.

Nothing seemed to go right for him that evening. First Pastor Reeves was gone. Then somebody else had beaten him to the library book he wanted to use for American history. He started to leave, but decided to wait for a while in hopes the book would come back in while he spent his time looking at college catalogs.

It was tough deciding on a school, he reasoned. Most of the catalogs sounded so much alike. There were fees to pay – so much per hour for tuition, and board and room. And there were the rules. Some schools were loaded with them. Some scarcely had any.

Jim had to think about his scholarship offer, too. If he went to State, he wouldn't have to work quite so hard or be so careful of his money. He'd be able to spend more time studying. And besides, Connie was going to be there. Or at least that was the way she talked. She had about given up going to the school in Wisconsin.

By the time he left the library that evening he had almost made up his mind to accept the scholarship and go to State.

On Monday after school, Jim reported to the gym for baseball practice. Coach Gardener was already there when he came in. As soon as the fellows got into their trunks and jerseys the coach called them together.

"I want you to start getting into condition first. Then we'll do a little throwing."

They did calisthenics and ran around the floor for fifteen or twenty minutes. When the session was over, they hadn't touched a baseball. For the first several nights Jim's muscles protested painfully. It wasn't long, however, until he was able to go through the entire routine without breaking into a sweat. It was the same with the rest of his teammates. Coach Gardener saw the change that was coming over the squad and nodded his approval.

"Next week I think I'll have the pitchers start to loosen up a little." He looked in Jim's direction. "We're going to depend a lot on you fellows this year." There was no missing what the coach meant.

CHAPTER 4

PUTTING THE PRESSURE ON

Jim was devoting all his spare time to baseball practice those days. He was down in the gym an hour before school and was back as soon as classes were over for the day. For the first week or so, Coach Gardener kept him from throwing as hard as he could. But as Jim got into condition he let him throw a little harder.

There were several pitchers out for the team and the coach gave them all a chance to show what they could do. It seemed, however, that the coach spent more time with Jim than he did with all the others put together. For fifteen or twenty minutes at a time he would stand behind Jim or the boy who was catching for him, watching every motion the youthful pitcher made.

"Try to follow through a little more, Jim," he said.

"OK. But that's sort of hard, Coach, when I have to hold back."

"I know." Coach Gardener nodded curtly. "How does the arm feel?"

"Great!" He grinned boyishly. "To tell you the truth, I'd like to fire in a few with some steam on them, just to see what it's like for once."

The coach reached over and patted him on the shoulder.

"That'll come. Right now, I want you to get the kinks out of those muscles and get in shape so you can throw hard without running the risk of pulling a muscle or ruining your arm." He started to walk away but turned back. "When we get through this afternoon, I'd like to see you in my office for a couple of minutes, Jim."

"Sure thing."

After practice, Jim showered and dressed hurriedly and went up to the coach's private office. Coach Gardener was there alone, waiting for him.

"Come in and close the door, Jim."

The boy did as he was told. Concern marked his young face.

"What's the trouble?" he demanded. "Am I down in English, or something?"

The coach shook his head.

"No, it's nothing like that, but if you've got a guilty conscience about your English grades, you'd better get to work on them. You and I'll have real trouble if you fool around and let yourself get ineligible."

"I think they're all right, only that's all I could think of that would cause you to call me in this way."

The baseball coach laughed.

"I just wanted to talk with you about a letter I just got from Gale Hanscomb." He paused briefly. "He wants to know what you've decided about going to State." The coach took the letter from his pocket and fingered it thoughtfully. "Time's running out, Jim, and Hanscomb is getting anxious to place his baseball scholarships." There was a long silence. "Tell me, Jim, have you decided what you're going to do?"

Jim felt his cheeks flush and sweat moisten his forehead. He ran his fingers over his face uncertainly.

"I–I don't know for sure," he said. There was hesitation in his voice.

Coach Gardener removed the letter from the envelope and opened it as though he was about to read it aloud but decided against doing so and put it away.

"I've got to write to Mr. Hanscomb tomorrow, Jim," he said firmly. "If you haven't told me by then, I'll have to assume you don't want the scholarship and will tell him so. We can't make him wait any longer."

Jim stiffened.

"Oh, don't do that!" he blurted quickly.

"But I have no choice. It isn't fair to State, to Mr. Hanscomb, or to the other boy who will get your scholarship if you turn it down. You'll have to decide by tomorrow if you want to go to State and play baseball."

Jim took a deep breath. He wanted to keep on talking, to explain the reason for his indecision, but as far as the coach was concerned, the conversation was over.

Jim's head swirled as he left the office and made his way down the steps and out to the parking lot where Fritz McCloud was waiting for him. His friend leaned over and opened the car door for him. For an instant he stared, as though he couldn't understand the indecision and bewilderment that had taken over Jim.

"What happened to you?"

Jim got in beside him and closed the door. "I just talked with Coach Gardener," he said woodenly.

Fritz gasped.

"You aren't ineligible or anything like that, are you?" he asked.

"I'm not ineligible, if that's what you're worried about."

His friend sighed his relief. "I'm glad for that. I thought at first that you were. And if that happens this year we won't have any baseball team."

Jim ignored his remark.

"It's about that State scholarship," he said. "I've got until tomorrow to decide whether I take it or not."

"That's easy," Fritz said. "All you've got to do is to tell him that you'll take it. There's no problem there, Jim."

"But it's not as easy as that. To tell you the truth I–I'm not at all sure that I want to take it."

Fritz' eyes widened.

"You've got to be kidding. You wouldn't turn down an offer for a baseball scholarship at State, would you?"

No answer.

"If you don't go to State with the offer you've got from them, you should have your head examined," Fritz retorted.

"Maybe so," Jim said, "but I still don't know for sure if I'm going there."

"For cryin' out loud! What kind of an offer would you have to have? Don't you know that Coach Hanscomb sends a player or two into pro ball almost every year? Everybody who knows anything about baseball says that he's one of the best coaches in the country."

"I know that," Jim acknowledged, "but there are a lot of things to think about when a fellow goes to picking a school."

They drove a couple of blocks without talking.

"Where would you go to college, if you didn't go to State?" Fritz asked finally.

"I've always thought I'd go to CBI."

"CBI?" Fritz' forehead wrinkled curiously. "What's that?"

"Cedarton Bible Institute."

Fritz' eyes widened.

"You mean to tell me that you're thinking about wasting your time going to a Bible institute?"

"That's where Danny and Kay went to school," Jim went on. "And they liked it really well. Ron and Darlene went there too."

"But your credits wouldn't be worth a thing," Fritz' voice rose. "The time you'd spend at a Bible institute would be wasted."

"I'm not sure where I'll go, Fritz."

They pulled up in front of Danny's home and stopped.

"Jim," Fritz went on, "I'd sure do a lot of thinking before I decided on going to a Bible institute, if I were you. Especially if I had an offer of a free ride through a top university like State."

"Don't worry. I'm going to."

Jim got out and walked slowly up to the front door. He had to decide about going to State or turning down the scholarship and going to CBI before the following afternoon. What was he going to do?

Jim didn't sleep well that night. Every time he closed his eyes he could see Coach Gardener's face, stern and questioning. He tried to pray, but there were times when prayer was almost impossible. He was so wrought up that night he could not bring himself to pray.

There was something else that kept him from prayer, something that he did not want to admit, even to himself. But it was there, nevertheless. He knew that all fellows and girls graduating from high school weren't led to Bible schools. Some were called to be witnesses in great universities and colleges across the country. Yet he wasn't among them. He couldn't bring himself to pray about the school he should attend, because he already knew what God wanted him to do. He had already felt the pull to go to Bible school and was resisting it. Praying would only make matters worse as far as he was concerned.

At last morning came and he got up and dressed. All he could think about was the decision he had to make that day regarding college. At noon he went down to the cafeteria and waited for Connie.

As usual, she was one of the last to arrive. She came hurrying, breathlessly, up to him.

"Hi, Jim," she exclaimed.

"Hi."

She saw the look on his face and her smile faded.

"What are you so glum about? You look as though you just flunked German."

"Right now, I feel that way," he told her. "I've got a problem – a real one!"

"So have I." She looked up at him. "At least it might turn out to be a problem."

They went into the cafeteria together and chose a table away from everyone else.

Connie paused momentarily.

"You knew Daddy has been wanting me to go to State, didn't you?"

Jim nodded.

"Well," she went on, "last night he put an application blank in front of me and practically made me sign it. He says that I have to go to State, if I'm going on to school at all."

Jim took a deep breath.

"I thought he was all for your going to some Christian school in Wisconsin."

"He was, but he's changed his mind about that.

Said that it costs more for one thing. And for another, State is so much better academically that he feels I should go there."

Jim stared at his glass of water thoughtfully.

"You said you had a problem that might be a problem, or something like that. What did you mean by that?"

Her smile was intended only for him.

"Silly! Don't you know what I was talking about? If you go to State it won't be a problem at all, but if you decide to go to CBI or some other Bible school it will be. Don't you see?"

Slowly Jim looked away. This made it even harder for him to decide.

They finished eating lunch and walked along the corridor together.

"So, you're really going to have to go to State," Jim said.

She nodded.

"I tried to get Daddy to let me wait about sending in my application until you made up your mind, but he won't let me put it off any longer. He said that all the good schools would be filling up and I wouldn't be able to get in anywhere, if I didn't apply now." Her eyes widened and grew luminous. "If you decide to go to CBI I won't say a word against it, Jim. I want you to do what the Lord wants you to, but I think I'd be the happiest girl in the world if you–" She stopped, blushing furiously.

Jim's heart beat a little faster. She must like him or she wouldn't be so anxious to go to the same school he was going to. He didn't know what he had ever done to deserve a girl like Connie. She was the sweetest, most attractive girl in all the world.

"It isn't that I wouldn't want to go to State, Connie," he said at last, his voice choking in spite of himself. "I think you know that. Going to the same school you go to would be the greatest. Only–" The words died in his throat.

Jim thought about the matter of college the rest of the day. Why in the world couldn't he make up his mind and then forget it? That was the way the other kids did.

When he finished baseball practice that evening, he went over to where Coach Gardener was standing.

"Well, have you made up your mind?"

He shook his head.

"That's what I'd like to talk with you about. Could I have another couple of days to think it over?"

Coach Gardener frowned.

"I'll give you until tomorrow. OK?"

That evening after dinner Pastor Reeves came over to talk with Jim. He had a CBI catalog in his hand.

"I've been wanting to have a chance to talk to you, Jim," he said.

"Oh, sure. Won't you sit down?"

There was an awkward silence.

"This is really none of my business, Jim," the minister said at last, "but if you haven't sent in your application to CBI yet, you'd better do it right away. Last year they had to turn away almost a thousand students because they didn't have any more dormitory space."

Jim stared at him. Color delicately etched his face and sweat moistened his forehead.

"I–" He picked up the catalog and looked at it.

"You know, CBI is an outstanding school," Pastor Reeves said.

Jim nodded.

"Yeah," he said curtly. "I know it is."

They talked about other things for a time before the minister excused himself to make another call. When he was gone Jim went into his bedroom and closed the door behind him.

Why did Pastor Reeves have to talk to him this particular day? Why did he have to come when he was already plenty mixed up as it was? It really wasn't Pastor Reeves' business whether he went to CBI, or State, or some other school. This was something he was going to have to decide for himself.

CHAPTER 5

DECISION MADE

Jim had some studying to do that night, but in spite of his efforts and the imminence of a stiff test, he couldn't bring himself to get at it. Instead, he picked up the Cedarton Bible Institute catalog once more and paged carelessly through it. Why couldn't he make up his mind where he wanted to go to school and forget the whole business? That was the way everyone else did. There wasn't anything he didn't know about either school that he would know the next morning. Why had he kept fooling around? Why hadn't he told Coach Gardener that he was going to go to State? That was what anyone else would have done.

He got to his feet and walked with measured steps to the window where he stared out onto the darkened street. The ache in his heart continued to grow. He shouldn't feel this way about choosing a school. He should be happy. Besides, wherever he went to school, he could serve the Lord.

Jim hadn't been standing there long when a sleek convertible went by. Idly he wondered if that was Robin's old car.

Why he thought of her he didn't know. He hadn't thought of her in months. But now the struggle she had in her Christian life came rushing to mind. She had faced a real turning point a few months ago. It had to be God's will for her life – or Alex Smith. And she had chosen Alex. As if that wasn't enough, she had gone away with him and had gotten married even before they graduated from high school. And she certainly wasn't happy. That was for sure. Neither was Alex. They'd made a terrible mess of their lives.

Jim thought seriously about it. Was he facing the same sort of thing? Was he facing a choice between allowing God to have first place in his life or playing baseball?

If he went to Bible school, it would mean that he wouldn't have a scholarship and would have to work that much more. And he would be giving up the fun and thrill of playing on a good intercollegiate baseball team. He'd have to get his enjoyment out of his Christian service assignment, whatever it happened to be.

He breathed deeply.

He knew that it wasn't wrong for a Christian to go to the university. He had known of too many fellows and girls who had been a powerful testimony for God in secular schools all across the country. But he knew too that his desire wasn't to go to State to witness and serve God. He wanted to go to make a name for himself on the baseball diamond. He wanted to have a chance of attracting the attention of professional baseball scouts in the hope that he might get a chance to work into the majors.

As Jim stood there, reflecting seriously, it was as though someone had suddenly turned a spotlight on the inner reaches of his heart to reveal something that wasn't right. Almost subconsciously he went back to his desk and fingered his Bible. Was he going to follow God's leading in his life? Or was he going to do as Robin had done and think only of pleasing himself?

In anguish Jim dropped to his knees and tried to pray. But there was no answer for him at the moment. When he got to his feet the ache within was as strong as before.

He went to bed and tried desperately to sleep but couldn't. There was no longer any doubt in his heart as to what God's will actually was for him. But what could he do about it now? How could he ever face Coach Gardener if he decided against the scholarship?

Miserably Jim threw his legs over the side of the bed and sat up. He turned on the lamp and reached for his Bible, but without even opening it a verse he had memorized some time long before came back to him. "I beseech you therefore…present your bodies a living sacrifice ."

Was he giving his body to God or to a game that meant a great deal to him? What good would all of the popularity in the world be for him if he was out of fellowship with the Lord?

In that instant Jim knew the decision he had to make. It didn't really matter what Coach Gardener thought of him. It didn't even matter if he wouldn't get to pitch another game for Fairview High. Even if Connie McCloud got so angry with him for his decision against State that she would never go with him again, God had to be first in his life. He had to go to Bible school!

Turning the pages of his Bible, he read aloud, "But seek ye first the kingdom of God, and his righteousness; and all these things shall be added unto you."

He knelt again. This time joy and peace flooded over him.

* * *

The following morning Jim told Danny and Kay about the decision he had made.

"We're so happy for you," Kay said smiling, "and so thankful that you decided to follow God's will for your life."

"That's right," Danny said. "The thing we've got to remember, is this. Whether you go to Bible school or State isn't the important thing. Many fine Christian young people go to secular colleges and universities and maintain a glowing testimony while they're there. The important thing is that God was calling you to CBI. And, that's where you should be going to school."

"It wasn't easy to make up my mind. Believe me."

There was a bounce in Jim's step as he walked to school. Now there were two other people he had to talk with – Coach Gardener and Connie McCloud. He wasn't at all sure they would respond the way Danny and Kay had. In fact, he was positive it would be just the opposite.

His steps slowed as he neared the corner where he and Connie usually met to walk to school. She was approaching from the opposite direction, a bright smile fighting her pretty young face.

"Hi, Connie."

"You look happy this morning," he said.

"Shouldn't I?"

"Oh, sure."

They started in the direction of the high school together.

"Did you decide about going to college?" Connie asked after a couple of minutes.

He nodded. "I guess it's going to be CBI."

She swallowed hard and it was a moment or two before she could speak.

"Aren't you making a terrible mistake, Jim?" she asked, tears lurking in her eyes. "You're throwing away a chance of a lifetime by turning down that baseball scholarship to State."

He shook his head. "No, Connie. I almost made the biggest mistake of my life when I seriously considered taking the scholarship. But I've finally got my thinking straightened out. With God's help I'm going to put Him first in my life." He breathed deeply. "I'm going to get my Bible school training. Then, if I decide I want to get a college education, I can go to college after that."

"But you'll be wasting those years of your life," she countered.

"I don't think studying the Bible can be considered a waste of time. No matter what kind of work I eventually go into, that study will always be helpful. Right now, the most important thing I can do is get good, sound training in the Word of God."

Connie's eyes flashed.

"I think studying the Bible is important too," she countered, "for kids who are new Christians or those who haven't been raised in Christian homes. But look at the Bible training you've already had from Danny and Kay and Pastor Reeves. You shouldn't have to worry about standing firm. If you can't do it with the background you've got, you can't do it at all."

Jim was a long while in answering her.

"That's the sort of thing I've been trying to tell myself," he went on. "Then I looked at Robin. When she got her car and started going around with Alex, she was going to win him to the Lord. It was about all she could talk about."

Connie's lips tightened as she waited for him to go on.

"Now look at Robin. She's married to an unsaved fellow and even has a hard time getting to church herself."

"I don't see what that has to do with you," she retorted, the hurt edging her youthful voice.

They talked about other things until they reached the school building, but as Jim left her to go to his locker, he knew that he hadn't made her understand.

It was the same when he talked to Coach Gardener.

"You're going to a Bible institute?" Contempt curled his lips. "If you'd told me that you had a better scholarship offer and were going to another university, I'd wish you well. But a Bible institute! I've never heard of anything so stupid."

Jim swallowed against the lump in his throat.

"I'm sorry to let you down, Coach. But I–I finally got the thing settled. I'm going to put Christ first in my life and do what He wants me to do."

Jim would have continued talking, but it was apparent that the baseball coach wasn't even listening. Hesitantly he left the coach's office and walked back to his homeroom. Coach Gardener hadn't mentioned their own baseball team. Maybe he wasn't even going to let him pitch anymore!

The thought was staggering, but it didn't really affect Jim. At least not the way he thought it would. The important thing was that he had finally been able to put first things first. He had turned his life completely over to God and was going to follow His will for his life.

* * *

Coach Gardener said nothing more to Jim in the weeks that followed about the university scholarship he had turned down. At first the boy was very much afraid he wouldn't be able to pitch for Fairview, but it didn't change things at all. He was still the number one starting pitcher and did so well in winning the first three games that he didn't have to be relieved. Scouts from other schools began to show up to watch him pitch, although he knew nothing about it until Coach Gardener called him aside and talked with him about it.

"I don't know whether it will do me any good to tell you this or not," he said, "but a couple of fellows from Wisconsin were here to watch you this afternoon, Jim. They were quite impressed by what they saw."

The boy's expression did not change. "Oh?"

Coach Gardener went over to a bench and sat down.

"They said they didn't want you to find out they were here until after the game was over. They were afraid it might make you nervous, if you knew they were watching you with a view to offering you a scholarship if you did well."

"That wouldn't make any difference to me now," Jim said evenly. "If I'd been wanting to take a baseball scholarship, I'd have taken the one Coach Hanscomb offered me. I couldn't have expected anything any better than that."

"You still haven't changed your mind about going to that–that Bible school?"

He shook his head. "I've already sent in my application to CBI," he answered. "I'm not interested in going anywhere else."

"That's what I told them. They said they wanted to talk to you anyway, but I said that it wouldn't do them any good. You'd already made up your mind."

"Thanks." A smile twisted Jim's face. "I really appreciate that."

There was a brief silence. The youthful pitcher would have gone on outside, but the baseball coach stopped him.

"Jim, there's something I've been wanting to tell you for the last week or so."

His eyes lighted curiously.

"I was pretty upset when you decided to turn down that scholarship from State. I felt that you had let me down, let Fairview down, and even yourself. I was positive that if you went through with your plans, you would be throwing your life away."

Jim tried to find words to answer him, but for the moment he could not.

"Then I got to paying particular attention to the way you conducted yourself on the baseball diamond and around school." For a long minute he paused, strumming the bench with his fingers. "You're different than the rest of the guys, Jim. You've got something they don't have."

Jim shifted uncomfortably from one foot to the other. "I–I–"

"The only thing I can see that might make you different is that you take this religion of yours seriously. All I can say is, 'Good Luck, Jim.'" He got to his feet and thrust out his hand impulsively. "State is not only losing a great baseball pitcher, but a real gentleman."

CHAPTER 6

DECISION CONFIRMED

That Sunday evening Jim appeared at church on a panel discussing the topic, "Should I go to Bible School?" Connie McCloud had come with him and was sitting in the second row from the front, her face white and drawn and her small hands trembling. Jim saw the anguish in her eyes and quickly turned away. Having her feel as she did didn't help any when it came to thinking about going to CBI. He felt worse about not going to the school she was going to than he did about having to give up the scholarship.

Pastor Reeves got to his feet after they had finished the preliminaries and introduced the subject to be discussed by the panel that evening.

"I don't know of any problem facing Christian kids getting out of high school today that is any more important than the one we're discussing tonight. The sort of school you choose can influence your entire life."

He paused and looked over the group thoughtfully.

"I'm not saying that each of you should go to Bible school or to a Christian college. Quite the contrary. There are undoubtedly some of you who are called to be witnesses on secular campuses. So the purpose of this discussion isn't to get you to decide to go to a Bible institute or Bible college. What we want you to do is to think seriously about the school you attend, and to consider God's will for your life when you make this important decision."

The discussion started out very much the same as other panel discussions. One of the sponsors asked a question to get the program under way. A girl who had been accepted by a Bible school in South Dakota told why she had chosen the school she did. A boy defended his reasons for going to the university on the grounds that the credits would be accepted any-where and by anyone. Then one of the senior fellows got to his feet and directed a question at Jim.

"You had a baseball scholarship at State offered to you, didn't you?" he asked.

Jim nodded.

"That's right."

"Then why is it that you decided on going to Cedarton Bible Institute?"

Jim took a moment or two before answering.

"While the others were talking," he began, "I've been sitting here thinking about that very thing. When I had a chance to go to State to play baseball,

I thought it was the most wonderful thing that had ever happened to me. I even got to thinking that I might be good enough to get a contract with the major leagues by the time I graduated."

He paused and looked about.

"I was really excited about going to State and playing baseball and making a name for myself."

"What would be so wrong with that?" somebody asked quickly.

"In my case, the thing that was wrong with it was that I wasn't taking the Lord into consideration at all. I was beginning to plan my life as though God didn't have a claim on me. But I didn't feel right about it. Every time I got to considering it, I got an uneasy feeling, as though I wasn't doing the right thing. I talked with Danny and Kay and Pastor Reeves about it, and prayed about it, and finally decided that the most important thing in all the world for me was to do God's will. So, I turned down the baseball scholarship and sent my application to CBI."

One of the fellows on the front row eyed him almost belligerently.

"Don't you think it's possible for a young person to be in the center of God's will and still go to a secular school like State? There are a lot of fine Christians going there. I happen to know some of them."

"I'm sure there are a lot of fine Christians going to the university," Jim replied quickly. "Like you, I've met quite a few of them. And I'm sure there are many who have actually been led to such schools for the ministry they can have among the non-Christian students."

"Then why didn't you take that scholarship? Think what you could have done for the Lord if you'd become an outstanding baseball player. Half the kids at State would be falling all over you."

"That would be fine," Jim said, "only that isn't God's will for me."

"What makes you say that?"

"The only answer I can give you is that I knew God didn't want me to accept that scholarship. Maybe He knows that my faith needs strengthening before going to a place where I'd be tested and tempted like some kids are in secular schools. Maybe He knows that I couldn't stand acclaim and success on the baseball diamond. Maybe I'd get to thinking more about myself and my ability and not about what He wants me to do. I don't know why He doesn't want me to go to the university and play baseball on a scholarship, but I'm finally willing to accept the fact that He doesn't and that His will is best for my life."

One of the girls on the panel spoke up.

"I think young people should consider going to Bible school for a couple of years to give the Lord a chance to speak to them about Christian service."

The moderator took up her statement.

"That's most interesting. Could you explain it a little more."

She breathed deeply.

"My brother went to a secular school for two years before he could accept the fact that God wanted him in Bible school, and he was miserable. It wasn't until Byron got to Bible school that the Lord was able to talk to him about the mission field. Now he's a missionary in Japan."

"That's wonderful."

But the girl had not finished. "The last time I talked with Byron we went over this matter of what school I was going to. He said that it was at Bible school that he started living close enough to God to make it possible for the Lord to speak to him about full-time Christian service."

The moderator got to his feet.

"That's a reason for going to Bible school that I've never heard before. But it is certainly legitimate. It's possible to fill our lives with so many activities that we aren't tuned to God's quiet voice."

They talked about that for a minute or two. Then one of the other fellows brought up a reason for not going to Bible school. It had been mentioned previously but nobody had picked it up.

"My folks say they want me to go to a school that is accredited, so I can transfer all my credits in case I want to go into teaching or something where I'll have to have a degree," he said. "They say Bible school is all right for someone who isn't going on to college, but otherwise it's a waste of important time."

Jim answered that question.

"That's one of the things that bugged me at first about going to CBI. The counselor at high school talked with me about it and this thing of credits seemed like a big deal. But then I got to thinking about it and talked to Pastor Reeves. He told me that he thinks this 'loss-of-credits' bit is overplayed. It depends on what field a fellow is going into, but he probably won't lose as much as he thinks he will. He told me about a fellow he knew who went to a Bible institute for three years before transferring to one of the best Christian colleges in the country. It took him two more years to get his degree. So, it took him a year longer than if he had gone to an accredited school in the first place."

The boy who voiced the objection spoke up.

"When you put it that way it doesn't sound like much, but the truth of the matter is that he lost a third of his time in Bible school."

Jim's gaze met his.

"I wouldn't say that studying the Word of God is a loss of time." The other senior stared at him without replying, so Jim continued. "Even if going to Bible school means that it's going to take me another year to finish my education, that's what I want to do. I'm convinced that it will give me a good, solid grounding in the Word of God, regardless of what I finally take up for a life's work."

When the evening service and panel discussion were over, Jim walked home with Connie. He was pleased with the way the discussion in the young people's meeting had gone and could scarcely think of anything else.

"It turned out to be a good youth program, didn't it, Connie?"

She glanced in his direction, and when she spoke her voice faltered.

"I–I guess so."

He noted the bite in her low tones.

"I hope I didn't make you feel bad by what I said," he continued. "I sure didn't mean to."

"Oh, no," she answered quickly – a little too quickly – it seemed to him. "It didn't make me feel badly. You're as entitled to your opinion as I am to mine. Only I don't think you were being quite fair."

Questions gleamed in his eyes. "About what?"

"About everything. Both of my parents went to secular colleges and they're good Christians. As good as you'll find anywhere. Just because someone decides to go to a secular school it doesn't mean that he's out of the Lord's will for his fife."

"I know that, Connie, but–" He was about to mention the careless attitude Mr. and Mrs. McCloud had toward the Lord's Day, and their attitude toward some things many Christians consider worldly, but he checked himself.

Not before Connie caught the inference, however.

"But what?" The ice in her voice grew apace.

"Oh, nothing."

"But what?" She was insistent.

Jim stopped and faced her.

"This isn't anything for you and me to start scrapping about, Connie," he said. "It won't be long until we'll be going to different schools and won't see each other or anything."

She nodded and her tone changed. "It makes me feel ill just to think about it."

He took a long breath and expelled the air slowly.

"You don't suppose there would be any chance of your getting to go to CBI too, do you?"

She shook her head. "I'm sure Daddy would never hear of it. He says he's going to have a hard enough time getting me through college without wasting any time going to Bible school."

"Maybe if Pastor Reeves would go to him and explain to him about the credits and everything, he'd change his mind."

"Not Daddy. When he makes up his mind about something, nobody can change it."

They started in the direction of the McCloud home once more, slowly, as though all the joy had been taken out of the evening.

"I–I'm sure going to miss you, Connie."

She did not reply immediately. It seemed to Jim that she was fighting to hold back the tears.

* * *

Graduation night at Fairview was a big occasion. Only a few weeks before Jim had been sure Danny and Kay would not be back from Guatemala in time to attend, and he felt worse about it than he would ever let anyone know. But they were back, seated toward the front of the auditorium and the Davis triplets were beside them.

After the diplomas had been presented and one of the local pastors had pronounced the benediction, Jim walked briskly to where Danny and Kay were waiting for him.

"Congratulations, Jim." Danny shook his hand warmly.

Doug Davis stepped up closer and put his hand on Jim's diploma. "I wish I had mine like that. I'll probably be in school a million years before I get one."

DeeDee looked at her brother.

"You might make it a little sooner if you'd study."

Jim nodded toward Danny, trying to get him off to one side so he could talk to him.

"What's the matter, Jim?" Danny asked. "Have you got problems already?"

"Problems? Oh, no–I mean–I–" He turned to see if Connie was still in the auditorium. "Danny, would you mind too much if I didn't go home with you this evening? I thought–"

Del Davis broke in to finish the sentence.

"I know what he wants to do. He wants to go out with that girl he's been making eyes at all night."

A crimson color crept up into Jim's cheeks. Danny tried to sound serious.

"Sure, Jim, we understand. You'd rather be with Connie than us."

"Oh, no, Danny. I mean–"

In spite of himself, Danny laughed.

"I told you we understand, Jim. Go ahead. Connie's waiting around just in case we OK this venture."

The two Davis boys looked first at each other and then at Jim.

"It's hard to believe one swell guy like Jim could go so crazy over a girl!"

"Yeah!"

Danny tapped the boy on the shoulder.

"You know, Doug, I used to think Jim would never show any interest in girls. Why, just a year ago last Christmas he was as disgusted as could be because Ron brought Darlene home with him. And then, suddenly, he grew up, displayed a little fuzz on his chin, and before I knew what was happening, he was eyeing the girls."

In spite of all the ribbing he was getting, Jim laughed as he turned and walked over to the other side of the large auditorium where Connie was waiting for him.

DANNY ORLIS AND THE DAVIS TRIPLETS' PROBLEM

CHAPTER 1

SAD NEWS

At the supper table Doug glanced impishly at Jim and then at Danny, who was sitting across from him.

"Say, Danny," he began, "who's that girl I always see chasing Jim?"

The color crept up into Jim's cheeks and he studied his plate as though it had suddenly become the most interesting object in the room.

Danny looked up.

"Which one?"

"I don't know. There's only one I can see. She follows Jim everywhere he goes, and she's always got a gooney look in her eyes. When she gets close to him, she rolls her eyes and says, 'Oh, Jim, you were just wonderful on the baseball diamond last night.'"

By this time Jim's face flamed crimson.

"Just you wait until I get you outside, Doug Davis. You'll be sorry."

The boy acted as though he hadn't even heard him.

"You should hear the way she gushes when she talks to him, Danny. It almost makes a guy sick just listening to it."

Del snickered. "You can say that again."

Everyone laughed except DeeDee.

"I don't think you and Doug are being very nice teasing Jim that way. Connie's a real nice girl and, after all, she's Jim's friend."

Del snickered again. "Jim's friend, eh? I hope I never get me a friend like that. If a girl followed me around that way, I think I'd sneak off where she couldn't find me, or leave the country, or something."

DeeDee's young mouth firmed. "I still don't think you're being very nice to Jim after the way he taught you to pitch and everything."

Doug spoke up. "You mean he *was* going to teach us to pitch. He hasn't had time because Connie wants him to go to the library with her. Or Connie wants him to come over to her house and listen to records. Or Connie has to study and he's going to help her. Boy, has she got him tied up!"

Del spoke up.

"That's right. And if we wait for him to find time to teach us to pitch, we'll be so old our beards'll get in the way."

Even Jim laughed.

"OK, just for that I'll take you out in the back yard

as soon as we finish devotions and start your pitching lessons. How does that sound to you?"

"Swell, but do you think Connie'll let you?"

* * *

The last of the week Dr. Kroeger stopped in Fairview on his way north to look over the mission stations in Canada. He stayed with Danny and Kay.

"Well, how are the triplets doing?"

Danny answered him. "Great. In fact, they're no trouble at all, except for the way they tease Jim and play tricks on him. And I don't think anybody minds that – including Jim."

"They're fine youngsters," the mission superintendent observed. "But what about their aunt? Have you heard any more from her?"

"I think she'll be coming to Fairview before long. We got a letter from her a few days ago. She wrote that she's beginning to feel much better. She seemed to think they would be able to come and get the triplets in a very short time."

Dr. Kroeger sat up straight and leaned forward slightly, lowering his voice. "I met a fellow the other day who knows Mrs. Roper and her husband," he said. "I certainly wish the kids didn't have to go down there to live."

Danny's eyes narrowed.

"If they aren't the kind who would make good

parents for the kids, maybe we'd better see if they really have to go to live with them."

"Oh, I didn't mean it that way," Kroeger replied. "At least as far as a judge would be concerned they would make fine parents. They will love them and see that they're well taken care of and will be taught certain moral values. But the home is worldly, so the triplets won't be getting any Christian training."

Danny nodded. "The kids have already been talking about that. They say that neither their aunt nor uncle is Christian."

Kay broke in. "They go a lot farther than that. They say that their aunt is definitely antagonistic to the gospel. Gerald and Rosalita tried to witness to them many times, but they weren't able to get anywhere."

Dr. Kroeger's lips pursed thoughtfully.

"That's one of the real tragedies of not providing for the Christian care of one's children in the event of the death of both parents."

"If Gerald and Rosalita had only left a will placing the children in the care of Christian friends, or even the mission, this sort of thing wouldn't be happening."

"That's right. And the worst of it is, the law is on their side. They're blood relatives of good moral standing and have money enough to provide a comfortable home for the children and see that they are well educated. There isn't a judge in the country who would even consider any other claim for the custody of the triplets."

Danny and Kay talked at length about the problem that night after everyone had gone to bed.

"I wish there was something we could do," Kay said.

"There isn't." Danny spoke firmly. "So, we'd just as well put the whole affair out of our minds."

"I can't believe that God would want those kids to go into an unsaved home when they're at such an impressionable age. Why, they could drift away and get into sin until no one would even be able to tell that they were Christians."

"Now, Kay, this isn't our problem. Remember? We've prayed about it, and this is the way God is working things out. So, we can't challenge it or say it isn't His will."

"Maybe not." She spoke slowly. "But I still don't think He wants those triplets to be raised in an ungodly home."

* * *

The following morning Kay was strangely depressed as she helped the triplets with their correspondence lessons. Del noticed her mood and asked her about it.

"What's the matter, Kay?" he began. "You sure don't act very happy this morning."

She managed a weak smile.

"What makes you say that?"

"I don't know, but you act sort of sad about something."

She did not answer him.

A short time later, Doug saw the mailman coming up the walk and ran to the door to meet him.

"We're getting some mail this morning, Kay," he called over his shoulder.

There was a letter, all right – a long, slim envelope with an airmail stamp. It was postmarked, "Texas." Kay's hands were trembling as she took it.

The triplets stood about her in silence as she ripped open the envelope and read the letter inside. In spite of herself, her face went ashen.

"What does it say, Kay?" Fear colored DeeDee's young voice.

Kay did not reply until Doug spoke.

"What do they have to say?"

"They–they're coming the last of next week–to–to take you back to Texas with them."

Although she knew she shouldn't cry in front of the triplets, the tears slipped, unheeded, down her cheeks.

* * *

Word that the triplets were going to be leaving spread rapidly throughout the Christian people in Fairview. On Sunday after church a large number crowded around them to tell them good-bye. They managed to answer when they were spoken to, but their faces were colorless and their usually dancing eyes were dull. At last, the crowd began to thin and Pastor Reeves came over to them.

"It's been so good to have you kids with us for a few weeks," he said. "We're going to miss you."

Doug swallowed hard.

"We're going to miss being here, too. I can tell you that much. If we had our way, we wouldn't be going down to Texas, even for a visit." His young voice was harsh with bitterness.

The minister nodded understandingly.

"I know just how you feel," he replied. "Our ways are not God's ways, and sometimes it's difficult for us to see just what He has in mind when He allows certain things to happen, but we can be sure that He has some purpose in all of this."

Del spoke up. "I suppose so, but I sure don't see what it could be."

"Perhaps not, but later you will probably understand. We'll probably all be able to see the reasons for it." He held out his hand. "We'll be praying for you."

"Th-th-thanks," Doug answered.

CHAPTER 2

LEAVE-TAKING

The last days the Davis triplets spent in Fairview with Danny and Kay passed far too rapidly for all of them. In the early part of the week, they worked hard to finish their correspondence lessons.

"I don't know whether we'll be ready to go into the next grade or not, Kay," DeeDee said.

"Oh, you should be," Kay told her. "You've been doing excellent work since you've been here."

"Sure." The girl had trouble continuing. "But that's because you've helped us and made us work on our lessons. I don't know if Aunt Carmen will have time to keep after us on our studies or not. She might not even care whether we get good grades."

Kay went over and put her arm about the slight, serious-faced girl.

"I wouldn't worry about that, if I were you, "she said. "Your aunt loves you so much that she and your uncle are coming all the way up here just to get you and the boys to go back and live with them. She's going to be as concerned about your studies as your mother and dad were."

DeeDee's lower lip trembled.

"You–you just don't know her. All she cares about is buying pretty clothes and going places and having a good time. She isn't going to be thinking about us and–and whether we have the things that are good for us or not."

Kay was still not convinced. "Oh, I'm sure you'll find her different when you are actually making your home with her."

DeeDee wiped the tears from her eyes.

"I wish we were going to stay with you and Danny," she blurted. "That's what I wish. I don't want to go down to Texas with Aunt Carmen. They don't go to church or anything."

* * *

Although Carmen Roper had written that she and her husband would get to Fairview on Thursday, the phone rang shortly after noon on Wednesday. Kay went to answer it.

"This is Carmen Roper." The voice had a faint Spanish accent.

Kay felt the muscles in her throat tighten.

"I–I–" She looked at the triplets who had gathered somberly around the telephone. They knew who she was talking with. That was apparent from the helpless look on their faces. "I–I mean, we didn't expect you quite so soon."

The woman on the other end of the line spoke breathlessly.

"That's why we stopped and phoned you. I know we're earlier than we wrote you we would be, but we're all so excited about having the triplets live with us that we decided to come a day early. I hope we're not inconveniencing you."

"Oh, no." Mentally Kay went over all the work she had yet to do. She hadn't finished cleaning the house and there were clothes to iron and pack. "It won't inconvenience us. It's just that I haven't gotten the triplets' clothes ironed and packed yet. I had planned on doing that in the morning."

"I'll help you."

"It won't take long."

"You've already done so much for the children," Carmen said. "Just leave the ironing and the packing. I'll help you with that when I get there."

Kay was trembling when she returned the phone to its cradle. For a moment or two, DeeDee and her brothers stared at Kay, their eyes wide and luminous. At last Doug spoke.

"That was Aunt Carmen, wasn't it?"

Kay nodded. Then she turned quickly and started for the kitchen. It would never do to let them see the tears in her eyes.

"I've got to have help from all three of you, if we're

going to get your things ready so we won't delay your aunt and uncle."

Del started to protest, but Kay began giving orders.

"Run down to the basement and get some clothes hangers, Del. And, Doug, you get the suitcases out of the garage, will you?"

Kay's eyes smarted as she worked, and the dread continued to grow in her heart. She masked her own apprehension and concern as best she could. It was hard enough for them, she told herself, without letting them see how she felt.

* * *

An hour or so later the Ropers pulled into the Orlis' driveway. Their car was one of the largest, most expensive makes in the country, and their clothes were of high quality. Carmen Roper, black-haired and very beautiful in her exclusive dress and coat, started to cry as she saw DeeDee and the boys.

"My darlings!"

She swept them into her arms.

"My darlings!"

Doug and Del stood there helplessly, staring straight ahead while she gushed over them.

"My poor sister's darlings!" With that she began to cry, sobbing until the mascara stained her olive cheeks. "You are going to come home with us now. We're going to take care of you."

At last she stopped crying and released the triplets from her embrace. She looked at Kay and managed a thin smile.

"I am so sorry, Mrs. Orlis." She held out her hand. "When I think of Rosalita, I–" Her voice choked once more.

"Won't you come in?" Kay smiled warmly. She introduced herself to Carmen's tall, sapling-thin husband, Clarence Roper, and their two children.

Philip was almost the same age as the triplets, only he was even darker than they were, and half a head shorter. Maria was a year and a half younger, a shy, slender wisp of a girl, as pretty as her mother. She smiled hesitantly up at Kay.

"Wouldn't you like something nice and cold to drink after your long ride?" Kay asked the girl.

Maria nodded wordlessly.

"We'll go in and see if we can find something in the refrigerator."

Philip sized up Doug and Del critically. It was a couple of minutes before he spoke to them.

"I sure am glad you guys are coming down to live with us," he said. They did not reply, but he acted as though he didn't notice. "The ranch foreman's got two girls. The cook's got a daughter, and the people on the ranch next to the Circle R have four girls." He wrinkled his nose distastefully. "They've got me surrounded."

Del nodded sympathetically.

"We know exactly what you mean," he said.

"We've got a sister, too."

Doug spoke up loyally.

"Of course, DeeDee isn't so bad to have around. She's a real sport. She's not like other girls."

"That's the way I feel about Maria. She's not like most of them – but she's still a girl."

While Kay made iced tea and lemonade, Carmen talked rapidly about her sister and the triplets.

"Clarence and I talked it over after–" She dabbed at her eyes again, "after we got word from this Dr. Kroeger about the–the accident. We decided that the least we could do for Rosalita would be to–to take her children and give them everything Rosalita would have liked to give them and–and couldn't."

Kay smiled understandingly.

"I'm sure your sister would be very grateful. Her children meant everything to her."

"I don't know." Carmen's expression changed slightly. "I don't know what came over Rosalita. When she went away to college she was–" She paused, groping desperately for words. "She was reasonable and–and well balanced. Then some organization got hold of her and she became so–so religious we couldn't even talk to her. She quit smoking and dancing and–" She shrugged her shoulders expressively. "In fact, she quit doing anything that was fun."

Kay smiled to soften what she was going to say.

"I wonder if you don't have the wrong idea of the sort of life Rosalita and Gerald lived, Mrs. Roper. They were as happy as anyone I've ever known."

But the visitor was not convinced.

"She couldn't have been happy." There was a tone of conviction and finality in her voice. "She and that fanatic she married didn't have a thing. She may have tried to put on an act about being happy, but she didn't fool me. She was as miserable as anyone I've ever known."

Kay looked into Carmen's grief-dimmed eyes and would have spoken, but her guest continued.

"Mother and I tried to talk Rosalita out of going into another church and marrying that religious fanatic she thought she was in love with, but the more we talked to her the more determined she was to have her own way." Her voice rose. "And he had to take her down to that terrible place to live among a bunch of–of dirty, lazy people who didn't think anything of them – who didn't even want them around."

Carmen began to cry once more. For a brief space of time, she fought to control herself, but without success. Kay went over to her and put an arm about her shoulders comfortingly.

"I know how terribly upset you are, Mrs. Roper. We can't understand why something like this should have happened, but it did. But the Bible tells us that 'All things work together for good to them that love God, to them who are the called according to his purpose.' We have to put our trust and faith in God."

She and Danny would be praying that the Lord would give them an opportunity to witness to Rosalita's emotional younger sister before they left, but this was not the time. She was too wrought up, too hurt to listen.

As Kay stood there, she prayed silently that God would be with this attractive woman and that in spite of the fact that she did not know Him as Savior, that He would give her strength and courage to carry on.

The Ropers were going to a motel on the edge of Fairview to stay that night, but Danny and Kay insisted that they stay with them.

"We wouldn't hear of your going to a motel," Danny said.

"We appreciate that, but you've done so much for us and the children already. We don't want to put you out," Clarence told him.

"You won't be putting us out. In fact, we'd feel terrible if you went to a motel."

"Well, I'll talk with Carmen about it," her husband said, "but we had already agreed that we were going to a motel. In fact, we almost stopped to register before coming over here."

"I'm glad you didn't."

It was finally decided that they would stay in the Orlis home. When Kay started to fix dinner, Clarence Roper informed them that he was going to take them all out to eat.

"That I insist upon," he concluded.

Philip and Maria talked excitedly to the triplets during the meal. DeeDee and the boys seemed to respond a bit. Soon they were laughing at the tales their cousin told of ranch life.

"You'll like it on the Circle R," he said. "We have lots of fun."

Doug grinned.

"You've been talking about all the fun you have, but you never say anything about the work. Don't you have any work to do?"

"Oh, sure," Phil said. "We work all the time – all the time we're not goofing around and having fun, I mean."

His dad leaned forward and pointed at Doug with his fork as he spoke. "Don't let him kid you. That's the only reason we want to get you down to the Circle R. We work all the time – seven days a week."

DeeDee's eyes widened.

"Don't you even go to church?"

Both Philip and Maria stared at her incredulously.

"Go to church?" Phil echoed. "Nobody around where we live goes to church. We don't have time for that."

Carmen glanced at Danny and Kay.

"We live so far from any church that it isn't possible to go every Sunday," she explained, suddenly embarrassed by the fact that they didn't go to church regularly. "But we go a couple of times a year. And when Philip and Maria go to high school, they'll also take confirmation."

For a moment or two the silence was strained. Then Clarence looked at his watch.

"Say," he said, "we're going to have to get a move on or we're not going to get to bed at a decent time tonight. And we've got a lot of miles to cover tomorrow."

They soon went home and by ten-thirty the Ropers excused themselves and went to bed. When Danny and Kay were alone the young pilot turned to his wife.

"Well," he said softly, "what do you think?"

Concern gleamed in her eyes. "I know they've got a legal right to the kids, Danny, but I'm really disturbed by their materialistic views and their lack of interest in anything that might be spiritual."

He nodded. "Of course, we expected that sort of thing. The kids told us what they were like."

Kay crossed to an easy chair and sat down.

"I'm very much disturbed at what might happen to the kids, Danny, but I must admit that in spite of all that I like Carmen and Clarence Roper very much. They seem like very fine people."

"I've been thinking the same thing. They're not at all the sort I expected them to be. From the way the kids talked I thought they would be terrible to get along with and might actually be mean to them."

"Oh, they'll be well treated. There's no concern in my mind about that."

A new note crept into Danny's voice. "We'll just have to pray for them."

The next morning Kay got breakfast for their guests at six o'clock, and by seven-thirty the car was packed and they were ready to leave. DeeDee and her brothers said good-bye tearfully.

"I–I sure wish we didn't have to go," the girl said, her lips trembling.

"We'll come down and visit you the first chance we get, DeeDee."

The girl dried her eyes and managed a weak smile.

"Do you think you can come this summer?"

"Well–" Kay paused uncertainly. "I don't know that we can come this summer, but we'll come there the very first chance we get."

Jim Morgan shook hands with Doug and Del, trying to hide the hurt in his heart behind a bantering laugh.

"Now you guys take it easy or they'll run you out of Texas."

"Fat chance."

Mischief glittered momentarily in Del's eyes. "Write to us, Jim," he said. "That is, if Connie leaves you enough time to write letters."

Jim scowled good-naturedly, turning to Clarence. "When you get these guys down on the ranch, Mr. Roper, will you dunk them in the stock tank for me? All they've done lately has been to give me a lot of static."

The lanky rancher laughed. "I'll tell you what I'll do. I'll dunk 'em twice. Once for you and once for that little gal of yours. How's that?"

Conversation lagged. They were all aware of the fact that the time had come for the triplets to leave. Carmen said good-bye to Kay.

"Do come and see us," she urged. "The children would love it and–and so would we."

Kay nodded in reply.

Clarence started the engine and in a moment, they were gone. Danny, Kay, and Jim stood in silence watching after the big, late-model car until it turned the corner and disappeared in the direction of the highway. For a time, no one spoke. At last Danny turned to his wife.

"I sure hated to see them go."

Kay could not speak. Jim picked up a twig and broke it in two.

"Well," Jim said, at last, "it sure isn't going to be the same around the house without those kids. They were great to have around."

Kay was crying softly.

CHAPTER 3

TRIPLETS' NEW HOME

It was a long, tiring ride from Fairview, Minnesota, to the Circle R ranch in southern Texas. At first the triplets talked and laughed with Philip and Maria, but as the day wore on, they lapsed into silence. DeeDee was especially quiet. Everyone noticed it.

"What is the matter, DeeDee?" Carmen Roper's accent was even more pronounced than usual.

"I'm all right."

"But you look so sad."

DeeDee fought a brief smile to her lips and held it there woodenly.

"I was just thinking about Kay Orlis. If we were back in Fairview with her and Danny, the two of us would be getting ready to go to the supermarket about now."

Her aunt was silent for a time.

"You like this Kay very much, don't you?"

DeeDee spoke quickly. "She's the grandest person I've ever known."

Carmen nodded seriously. "She must be a very good person to take care of you and the boys the way she did."

DeeDee choked on the lump in her throat and turned quickly away so Carmen would not see that tears still lurked in her eyes. Kay was more than just a very nice person, she was the next thing to her own mother. But how could she tell her Aunt Carmen that?

It was long after dark the third day when they pulled into the ranch yard and stopped. Clarence switched off the lights and got out of the car.

"Well, we're here."

Doug and Del stirred sleepily.

They took in only the suitcases which had their pajamas and the things they would need for that night. DeeDee shared a room with Maria and Doug and Del were to bunk in with Philip.

"If this is not all right," Carmen said, "we'll fix something else tomorrow."

DeeDee flashed her aunt a quick smile. "Oh, I'm going to like being in the same room with Maria. I wouldn't want to be alone."

Doug spoke for both himself and his brother. "Being in with Phil suits us fine, too."

They were all so tired they tumbled into bed and fell asleep without talking at all.

It was almost ten o'clock the next morning when

they awoke. Clarence was standing in the doorway looking at them when they finally opened their eyes.

"Well, are you going to sleep all day?"

Del scrubbed at his eyes with his fist as he swung his feet over the side of the bed.

"You'd better hurry. Breakfast is ready."

At the breakfast table a few minutes later, the triplets bowed their heads and waited, but no one asked the blessing. Clarence reached for the bacon.

"Here, Doug," he said, "help yourself and pass it to–" He stopped curiously as he saw that the boy had his head bowed and his eyes closed. "What's goin' on here, anyway?"

Doug looked up. "We were waiting to ask the blessing," he explained. "Don't you do that before you eat?"

Clarence's forehead wrinkled. He started to say something, but Carmen spoke up quickly.

"Would you like to say the blessing, Douglas?"

He bowed his head once more. "Dear God," he prayed, "thank You for watching over us and helping us to get here safely. Now bless this food and help us to put our faith and trust in You. Amen."

The simple prayer seemed to choke off the conversation. And when they finished eating Clarence sent the kids outside.

"I want to talk with your mother for a minute, Phil," he said. "You take the kids outside and wait for me. There's something I want to show you when I get around to it."

When they were gone, he turned to Carmen.

"What do you think of that?" he asked, disapproval clouding his voice.

She did not answer him.

"That's not going to happen again," he said. "Why, I'd be the laughingstock of this end of Texas if that happened when we had guests."

Carmen's gaze met that of her husband and held there. "I don't like the idea of having them praying at mealtime any more than you do," she said, "but what can I do about it?"

"I don't know what you'll do." His voice was harsh. "But I can tell you this much; we've got to do something. It's not going to happen again!"

She laid a hand on his arm. "I'll talk to them about it, Clarence," she promised. "I'll see that they don't keep on praying at the table. But I'd rather not say anything about it to them right now."

"Why not? There's no better time that I know of to put a stop to it."

"Everything's strange here and they're still so–so upset about losing their parents. I don't want to hurt them any more than they've already been hurt, for a little while at least."

He frowned his disapproval. "I don't see why you have to make such a big deal about it. All you've got to do is tell them that I don't like it and that it can't happen again. That shouldn't give them any trouble."

"But you know how Rosalita raised them. They've

been so religious all their lives they probably think it's a terrible sin to eat without saying a prayer."

The tall rancher swore. "I can tell you this much. Now that they're here, they're going to get some of that religion knocked out of them. I'm not going to stand for it."

Nevertheless, when he went outside, he said nothing to the triplets about it.

"Well," he began, smiling genially, "what do you think of the ranch?"

DeeDee answered him. "It's awful big."

"Just wait until you get to riding over it. Then you'll begin to get an idea of just how big it really is." Pride kindled in his voice. "Do you know, you can ride horseback for three hours in any direction and still be on our land?"

Del whistled his amazement.

"That's what I like to do best," Phil said, breaking in quickly. "I like to go horseback riding. How about you guys?"

Doug frowned. "That's something I've always wanted to do, but I've never had a chance to."

"You'll get plenty of chances to ride around here," their cousin said.

DeeDee turned to him. "How about me? Will I get to ride, too?"

"Oh, sure. Even the girls ride here."

Clarence spoke up.

"That's what I wanted to talk with you kids about this morning," he said. "Let's walk down to the horse barn. I have something there I want to show you."

They went along with him, curious. At the barn door he stopped.

"Everybody around here has a horse of his own," he said.

They stared at him incredulously.

"You mean–you mean we're going to have horses to ride?" Doug asked.

"Better than that. I've decided to give each of you a horse of your very own."

Their eyes lit suddenly.

"I was going to let you pick them out this morning," their uncle went on, "but I've changed my mind. I think I'm going to have you learn to ride first. Then I'll give you each a horse with some life – a horse that'll let you keep up with Phil and Maria when they go riding."

"Boy, that's great! I've always wanted a horse of my own!" Doug said. "But I really didn't think I'd ever have a chance even to learn to ride."

"Well, once you've learned to ride without falling off, we'll teach you to handle a rope so you can help us with the branding and work around the ranch. We'll make real cowboys out of you yet."

Phil turned to Del. "See, what'd I tell you? You're going to be crazy about living with us on the Circle R. After you've been here for a couple of months, you won't want to go back to Minnesota for anything."

Clarence began saddling three of the more gentle

horses on the ranch for the triplets to use until they learned to ride.

"Have you done any riding before?" he asked.

They shook their heads. "We've never lived where there were horses to ride."

"There's really nothing much to it, but it's important that you don't get scared and that you get started right."

Philip spoke up quickly. "The main thing is practice, and you'll get plenty. Maria and I'll see to that."

Their uncle showed them how to mount and had DeeDee try first.

"One thing that's very important is to be calm and deliberate in everything you do with your horse. That will let him know exactly what you expect of him and will give him more confidence in you."

DeeDee giggled nervously. "I'm glad somebody has confidence in me. I–I'm scared to death."

"Now, take hold of the saddle horn with your left hand, put your left foot in the stirrup and swing up into the saddle."

"Like this?"

"That's right. You did fine. See, there's nothing to it."

He had her dismount and mount several times before turning his attention to one of the boys. Satisfied at last that they knew how to get on and off correctly, he had them walk their horses around the yard.

"You're doing fine," he said reassuringly. "Keep up the good work."

* * *

For the remainder of the week Clarence had them riding two or three hours each day. It wasn't long until they were riding like veterans. They would swing up on their ponies the way Phil and Maria did and go galloping off at top speed. Clarence watched approvingly.

"Well," he said, "what do you think of riding now?"

Doug and Del both beamed.

"It's great! I don't know of anything I've ever done that was more fun."

"Wait until you get a good horse under you. Then you'll find out what fun is."

"We've been wondering when we were going to get those fast horses you've been telling us about."

The rancher laughed. "Just keep your shirts on, fellas. You've still got a few things to learn before you're ready to get another horse."

"We're sure getting anxious."

Clarence went over to Del and took hold of his horse's bridle.

"I've got a little proposition to make you."

The boy eyed him quizzically. "What's that?"

"The people out here in Texas are a little different than those where you used to live." He spoke hesitantly, as though he was not exactly sure what words to use.

Del nodded. "Most of the people where we used to live couldn't even speak English," he said.

"That's not quite what I meant. The people around here are wonderful, and in their way, they're religious. But they don't do things the way you do."

By this time DeeDee and the boys were listening intently.

"I–I don't know what you're driving at," Del said.

Their uncle laughed shortly. "Oh, it's not very much. I'm sure you never thought how it might look to other people. But I'm talking about the way you say a prayer before we eat."

DeeDee's eyes widened. "You mean you don't want us to ask God's blessing on the food?" she asked incredulously.

"It isn't that I don't want it," he said, fumbling lamely for words. "It doesn't make a lot of difference to me one way or the other. But I've been wondering how it's going to look when some of our friends come over who aren't used to anything like that."

"Dad and Mother always asked the blessing before they ate, no matter who came to visit," DeeDee said.

"That's just it. They could do it because they're missionaries and people expected it of them. But I'm a rancher."

DeeDee still was not persuaded. "It wouldn't have made any difference to Dad and Mother about that. They still would have prayed before they ate."

The rancher's face was scarlet. "I don't think they would have if they were in my position. What I've been trying to tell you is that I'll make a deal with you. If you'll stop praying at the table, I'll give you each a good horse."

The kids stared at him as though they could scarcely believe that they had heard him correctly.

"Of course, I don't have to make a deal like that with you if I don't want to. I could just tell you not to pray at the table anymore." Anger smoked across his lean face. "My friends wouldn't like it and I don't like it, so I want it to stop. If there's any praying to be done at the table, I'll do it! Understand?"

With that he stormed away.

Phil turned slowly to his cousins.

"You'd better not pray out loud at the table anymore," he warned. "When Dad gets mad like that, watch out! He'll clobber you!"

The kids rode for an hour or so after that, but somehow, they didn't enjoy it. And as soon as one of the girls suggested they quit for the day, they all rode to the barn and unsaddled. Phil had an errand to run, and Maria went off with DeeDee, leaving Doug and Del alone.

"Was I ever surprised when Uncle Clarence exploded about our asking the blessing at the table," Doug said. "I didn't even know it really mattered to him, did you?"

Del shook his head. "Aunt Carmen mentioned it yesterday or the day before, but she didn't act as though it was anything that bothered her."

Doug climbed up on the corral fence and sat down. Del joined him.

"What do you think we should do about it?"

His brother spoke up quickly. "I don't know about you, but I'm going to follow Phil's advice. I don't want to have trouble with Uncle Clarence."

There was a long silence.

"I was just beginning to like it here."

"Me, too."

Doug got off the fence and stood motionless, looking uneasily across the prairie.

"Danny was talking about how it might be hard for us to live a Christian life here," he said, as though he was talking to himself. "But until this afternoon, I didn't think he knew what he was talking about."

CHAPTER 4

PROBLEMS ARISE

That evening as the boys were getting ready for bed, they were unusually quiet. Doug made his way to their bedroom window where he stood for a long while. Finally, Del spoke. "What're you thinking about?"

"Uncle Clarence." His voice was low and guarded.

"That's what I thought. I still can't get over it. I didn't think he'd be so angry about our praying at the table."

"Neither did I." He turned to face his brother. "And I'm afraid this is just the start of it. It's sure going to make things tough for us."

"Oh, I don't know," Del replied. "All we've got to do is to quit asking the blessing since that makes him so mad. Outside of that, he's a swell guy."

Doug went to the desk and sat down.

"That's not what I meant. I was thinking about living a Christian life in a place like this. It's going to be tough if we can't go to church, or ask the blessing at mealtime, or have family devotions every day."

The corners of Del's mouth tightened. "We can't let that make any difference, Doug. We've got to live the way a Christian should live. We've got to do the way the folks would want us to."

"But how can we keep being the kind of Christians we should be?"

There was a short silence.

"Well, in the Bible, Daniel and his friends stayed true to God. They were taken to a different country and made captives. Nobody else in the king's palace worshiped the true God, but that didn't stop them from worshiping God in the way they had been taught at home."

"I know all that." Irritation tinged his voice. "And it's easy enough to say what we're going to do and not do. But it's entirely different when the time comes that we've got to do it."

Del leaned forward eagerly. "I know all that. But we don't have to do it alone."

Doug ran a hand across his face. "We're not going to find anyone around here to do anything to help us live the sort of Christian life the folks would want us to live. That's for sure."

"But we can ask God to help us," Del reminded him. "He's already promised to do that."

The boy paused momentarily. "I know that, and I believe it, but what can we do to help ourselves? That's what I've been trying to figure out."

His brother turned the matter over thoughtfully in his mind.

"Uncle Clarence can stop us from praying at the table," he said at last, "but he can't stop us from having devotions together every day."

"That would help, all right."

"And maybe we could work out some sort of a little service on Sundays, just you and me and DeeDee, to take the place of church."

"Hey, that's an idea."

Del's eyes brightened suddenly. "And there's something else we can do. We can listen to one of the Christian radio broadcasts the way we did with the folks in Guatemala. The broadcasts were our church services when we lived there."

Doug nodded. "But do you think we'll be able to pick up any broadcasts like that out here."

"Oh, sure. You can find them anywhere in the country."

Doug took a deep breath. "Boy, when you stop to think of it, there are really a lot of things we can do to help us live close to God even though we can't go to church or ask the blessing at the table."

* * *

Maria wasn't feeling too well that evening and had gone to her room, so DeeDee was helping her Aunt Carmen with the dishes alone.

"It's so nice to have you here, DeeDee," the older woman said. "You're a good example to Maria. You show her how to work. I'm afraid she doesn't like to do dishes very well."

"I didn't like to do dishes, either, when I was Maria's age, but there was always so much to do in Guatemala that we all had to pitch in and hold up our end of things."

Carmen laid the dish towel aside and turned to her attractive young niece.

"It's so hard to think that your mother is–is no longer alive," she said. "Sometimes I wake in the night and–and cry for her."

DeeDee fought back a tear. "We miss her and Daddy very much, but they're in heaven now and that's so much better for them. They have no sickness or worries or sadness. Everything is happy and–and wonderful."

A strange, wistful longing gleamed in Carmen's black eyes. "I hope I live good enough to go to heaven someday," she said.

"Oh, you could never live a good enough life to get to heaven."

Briefly Carmen's temper flared. "It's not nice to say such things," she scolded. "I think I'm as good as this–this Kay Orlis."

"Oh, I didn't mean it that way, Aunt Carmen. I was just thinking of some Bible verses that Mother taught me; some verses that say no one can live a good enough life to get to heaven."

Her aunt frowned. "But I don't do bad things," she protested. "I try very hard to live a good life so I can go to heaven."

"The Bible says that isn't good enough. It says, 'There is none righteous, no, not one.' And in another place it says, 'The wages of sin is death.' That means that none of us live without sin, and that if we sin then we've earned death and deserve to go to hell."

Her aunt's dark cheeks went ashen.

"I–I–"

At that moment Maria came into the kitchen.

"Mother, I'm hungry," she said. "I'm awful hungry."

Carmen stopped what she had been doing and went over to her.

"Do you think you feel like eating?" she asked.

The girl nodded. "My stomach feels a little better now. I thought maybe some milk toast would taste good."

"You go back to bed," her mother ordered. "I'll fix it for you and bring it to you in a few minutes."

"But–"

Her mother's voice rose. "Go back to bed!"

Reluctantly the slight, dark-haired girl turned and left the kitchen. Her mother waited until she had time to get to her room. Then she turned to DeeDee, her face harsh.

"Don't you ever talk to Maria about the things you have talked to me about tonight, DeeDee. Do you understand?"

The girl took half a step backward, involuntarily. "Don't you want her to become a Christian and go to heaven?"

Carmen jerked upright.

"I mean it, DeeDee. If you talk to her just once, I'll have your Uncle Clarence deal with you! We're not going to have her becoming the same sort of fanatic you and your brothers are!"

DeeDee's throat choked, and she swallowed miserably. As soon as she finished drying the dishes, she went to the bedroom she shared with Maria and sat down at the desk. The girl in bed sat up, curiously.

"What're you doing, DeeDee?"

"I thought I'd write to Danny and Kay."

She turned back to the desk, but not before Maria saw the desperate hurt in her eyes.

"What's the matter, DeeDee?"

"I–I'd rather not talk about it," she retorted, "if it's all the same to you."

The younger girl scooted out of bed and came over to her. "You can trust me, DeeDee. I won't tell anybody. I won't give your secret away."

At that there was a brief knock and the door opened. Carmen came in.

"Here's your milk toast, Maria."

Although she was talking to her daughter, she stared intently at her young niece.

"Eat this, my dear. I think it will help settle your stomach." Her gaze came back to her daughter briefly, then returned to DeeDee. "Then I think DeeDee had better come into the other room so you can get to sleep."

"But–" Maria started to protest.

"It will do you no good to argue, Maria." Her voice was clipped and decisive. "Eat and go to sleep. Tomorrow you'll feel better."

She went to the door and stood there until DeeDee got up and went out into the other part of the house.

"You didn't say anything to Maria about that religion of yours, did you?"

DeeDee shook her head. "Good. See that you don't." Her eyes were dark with warning.

DeeDee sat down in an easy chair near the lamp and picked up a magazine. She still had not opened it when Carmen came in with a checkers game in her hand.

"How would you like to play a game of checkers?" she asked, her entire manner changing.

"I suppose it would be all right." The girl spoke listlessly.

"It's been ages since I've had a good checkers game."

They set up the board and began to play. Clarence watched them for a time before drifting off to another part of the house to read. DeeDee tried to keep her mind on the game, but it was not easy. All she could think about was the change that came over her aunt and uncle every time the gospel was mentioned.

They were both nice enough, she had to admit. In spite of the way they acted about anything Christian, she liked them both. And she knew that they liked her and the boys. They had taken them in and had made a home for them exactly as though they were their own children. There wasn't anything different in the way they were treated, that she could see. They had the same kind of clothes Phil and Maria did. They got the same kind of gifts. Uncle Clarence was even going to give them horses that were as good as those his own kids rode.

DeeDee knew that she and the boys should be thankful for a home like this. They might have had to go to an orphanage somewhere, or be separated and never get to see each other again.

If only they weren't so bitter against the gospel. If only they would let her and her brothers do what they knew they should do to keep close to the Lord.

Carmen looked up from the board.

"DeeDee," she said, her voice softening.

"Yes?"

"It's your turn."

"Oh." Color crept up into her cheeks. "Oh, I'm sorry."

"I hope I didn't upset you by what I said just now."

"It did bother me some," she admitted candidly.

Carmen reached out and took the girl's hand in her own. "I'm sorry if I upset you. I didn't want to do that. I–I just wanted to get the record straight so there wouldn't be trouble between you and your Uncle Clarence."

CHAPTER 5

FUTURE BRIGHTENS

It was almost ten o'clock when Carmen and DeeDee quit playing checkers.

"I think I'll go to bed now," DeeDee said, getting to her feet.

"That sounds like an excellent idea." Carmen smiled warmly. "But be quiet when you go into your bedroom so that you don't wake Maria. I want her to be sure and get her rest."

DeeDee went into the bedroom as quietly as possible. She got ready for bed without turning on the light, but as she crawled into bed Maria rolled over and sat up.

"DeeDee?" she whispered.

"Quiet. You're supposed to be asleep."

"I've been waiting and waiting for you to come to bed. I thought you were never coming."

The older girl did not answer.

"What were you and Mother talking about when I came into the kitchen earlier this evening?" she asked.

DeeDee swallowed hard and did not reply to her question.

"What were you talking about?" she persisted.

"I–I–"

"I won't tell her," she said softly. "Honest, I won't. I won't tell anybody."

"I'm sorry, Maria, but I can't tell you anything about it."

"You don't have to worry about me. I can keep a secret."

"That isn't it," DeeDee said. "Your mother made me promise that I wouldn't talk with you about it, so I can't. That's all there is to it."

Maria leaned forward. "It was about your religion, wasn't it?" she asked pointedly.

DeeDee gasped. "Who told you?"

"Nobody." There was triumph in her voice. "I figured it out for myself. I got to thinking about how upset Mother was when you finished, and that made me remember hearing her and Daddy talking about your religion. They sure don't like it."

DeeDee sat facing her younger cousin. She couldn't say anything about Aunt Carmen or Jesus to Maria. Her aunt had made her promise that she wouldn't.

"What did Mother say about your religion?" Maria went on.

"I–I can't tell you anything," DeeDee replied lamely.

"Why don't they like it?" There was a curiosity in her voice that had never been there before. Whenever Aunt Rosalita and Uncle Jerry would come here, Mother and Daddy would get so mad about their religion they–" Her voice trailed away. "I'm sorry. I didn't mean to say anything about your folks. I–I didn't even think."

"That's all right." DeeDee managed to smile.

"I can't understand it at all. Why would they get so mad about religion? It's supposed to be something good."

DeeDee spoke slowly. "All I can say, Maria, is that I think maybe they're afraid you'd become like Doug and Del and me if we talk to you about God."

The younger girl's face crinkled. "That can't be it. They say you are the best kids they've ever seen."

DeeDee had no answer for her. How could she tell Maria why her mother objected to having her hear about Jesus – how He died for sin so she could be saved by confessing that she was a sinner and putting her trust in Him. She wasn't even sure herself why such talk made Aunt Carmen angry. And besides, would she dare to say anything, knowing how angry it would make both Aunt Carmen and Uncle Clarence, even if she hadn't promised to remain quiet?

"I think we'd better go to sleep, Maria," she said sternly. "Your mother's apt to hear us talking, and if she comes in and finds that you're still awake, we'll both be in bad trouble."

The younger girl lay back down and closed her eyes.

"All right," she said, "but it sure makes me curious

to know what there is about your religion that would make Mother and Daddy so afraid of it they don't even want you to talk about it."

DeeDee did not say any more, but for a long while she prayed silently for her aunt, uncle, Phil, and Maria that they would finally listen to the gospel and make their decisions for Christ.

She wanted to tell Doug and Del what had happened between her and Aunt Carmen, but she did not. It would only make them feel bad and they had enough problems already.

The next morning when they got up it was as though Aunt Carmen had never said anything to her. She was as sweet and cordial as she had ever been in her life. Even the boys noticed it and teased DeeDee about being Aunt Carmen's pet.

* * *

The triplets rode their horses every day as soon as they finished the chores that were given to them to do. Clarence didn't say anything to them about the way they rode, but he noted their progress as horsemen with growing satisfaction. Without making an explanation he took away the horses he had let them learn on and gave them others. Their new mounts were gentle but had a great deal more life. They could run at a hard gallop without getting winded, coming much closer to being able to keep up with the horses Phil and Maria had.

"Are these the saddle ponies your dad promised to give us when we learned to ride?" Del asked.

Phil shook his head. "Nope. You've passed the first tests and he's giving you some others."

"It's a lot more fun to ride these horses," Doug put in.

"Yeah, it's little better than what you used to have. But they still aren't what a fellow would call good horses. I went out with him the other day and helped him pick some out. He's got some real saddle ponies lined up for you as soon as he thinks you're ready for them. They've got plenty of life."

"This horse has all the life I'd ever want," DeeDee said. "I'd probably be scared to death if I got on one that could go any faster."

Maria broke in quickly. "You say that because you haven't had the experience to feel confident on a good horse. And you haven't ridden a pony that can get out and move. When you do, you'll see that these are just old plugs."

"I wasn't going to tell you, but I guess it won't make any difference," Phil went on. "Dad's got some trained cow ponies for you. You can rope off them, or herd cattle, or anything."

Del could scarcely believe it. "You aren't kidding, are you?"

"No, I'm not kidding. He wants you to have good cow ponies so you can help with the work on the ranch. He says you'll be able to do a lot of things before the summer is over – things that'll really be a big help to him."

Del's and Doug's eyes gleamed with excitement.

"That's something I've been dreaming about," Doug said, "but I didn't know whether it would ever happen or not."

DeeDee spoke up. "What about me?"

"You'll get your chance, too," Maria said. "I help with the work around the Circle R, and Daddy says I'm going to be able to help more than ever this year."

"I can hardly wait! You know, it's going to be a lot of fun helping herd cattle and brand calves at roundup time."

Phil grinned.

"You can say that again. It's a lot of fun. An awful lot of fun. But a guy can get tired of it after a while."

Del was not convinced. "Maybe you get tired of it, but I won't. I'll never get tired of it."

"Oh, yes, you will," Phil said. "There were a couple of times last year when I was so tired of working on the roundup that I'd have given most anything to get out of it."

Maria snickered. "Phil was so tired last year that he went to sleep at the supper table and Dad had to carry him up to bed."

The rancher's son felt his cheeks tinge with color. He looked away until somebody changed the subject.

Clarence did not wait until the triplets had their own cow ponies before putting them to work. One morning after they finished taking care of their horses, he sent them out to ride fence.

"You can take the boys with you, Phil," he said, "and ride the fence around the north pasture."

"OK, Dad."

"It's a long ride. You'd better take along some sandwiches for lunch and a couple canteens of water."

His son nodded.

At that moment Maria broke in.

"What can DeeDee and I do?" she asked. "Have you got some fence we can ride?"

He thought momentarily.

"There's always fence to ride, but you wouldn't be able to fix it, if you did find a break."

"Maybe not, but we'd know where the fence is down. We could take Phil and the boys right to the places they'd have to fix."

He smiled.

"I guess you've got something, at that." He turned to face the smaller pasture that lay just west of the house. "You can ride the fence around that pasture, Marie. But be sure to remember where the breaks are."

The girl's eyes gleamed.

"You can count on us, Dad."

The girls got back shortly before noon, but it was almost suppertime before Phil and the Davis boys returned. Maria and DeeDee went down to the barn to see them as they unsaddled their mounts and fed and watered them.

"We didn't find a single break in the fence." There was disappointment in DeeDee's voice.

Doug laughed. "We knew you wouldn't. That fence was just fixed a week ago."

Her eyes widened. "Was it, really?"

Phil was the one who answered her.

"No, it wasn't. To tell you the truth, we didn't find any breaks, either. Dad's mighty particular about his fences. They're checked so often that we find the trouble before it gets very bad."

DeeDee made a face at her brother.

"Oh, we were just going to have a little fun with you, DeeDee," Doug said.

She started to speak but stopped and looked at her watch. Then she looked up at her brothers guardedly.

"It's about time for it."

Maria and Phil eyed her curiously.

"Time for what?"

She did not answer him directly.

"We'd better hurry, Doug."

Maria grasped her by the arm and subconsciously lowered her voice to a whisper.

"What is it, DeeDee? Time for what?"

"Yeah," Phil broke in. "What are you talking about? What is it about time for?"

Doug glanced over his shoulder to see if anyone else was close enough to overhear what they were saying.

"Well–"

DeeDee spoke up quickly. "Doug, you know what Aunt Carmen said. She told us we shouldn't say anything to either Maria or Phil."

"Shouldn't say anything about what?" Phil Roper persisted.

"You don't have to worry about Mother," Maria giggled. "She makes a lot of noise, but she never does anything."

"I don't know," DeeDee said uncertainly. "She acted as though she'd do plenty to me."

There was a brief hesitation.

"She won't, if she doesn't know anything about it."

DeeDee frowned.

"I only promised I wouldn't talk to you," she said. "Nothing was said about listening to the radio."

"Listening to the radio?" Phil echoed. "Is that all you're going to do? I thought maybe you had something exciting planned."

Doug turned to his cousins. "If we let you listen to this program, you've got to promise not to tell your folks."

He led the little group around the barn, out of sight of the house, and turned on the radio he had been carrying. The announcer was just introducing the start of the Christian broadcast they tried to listen to every day.

Phil took hold of Doug's arm. "Is this what you were talking about?"

He nodded. "We've tried to get out to listen to it every afternoon."

"So that's what you've been doing," Maria said.

"We wondered what happened to you about this time every day."

DeeDee reached over and turned the volume up slightly.

"Sh. I want to hear the program."

Maria's young face reflected her indignation. "What kind of a joke are you trying to pull on us, anyway?"

Del answered her. "It's no joke. We listen to this broadcast regularly because we don't have any church to go to."

DeeDee spoke again.

"Sh."

The little group fell silent and crowded about the radio, listening intently.

When the program was over, Doug switched it off. For the space of half a minute or so nobody spoke.

"That's the first time I've ever heard anything like that." There was a strange wistfulness in Phil's voice. "How long has it been on?"

Del was the one who answered.

"I wouldn't know, but it's been on for a long, long time."

Phil thought about what the speaker had said.

"Is that the same religion your folks believed?" he asked.

"That's right."

Phil would have said more, but his father came around the corner of the barn just then.

"There you kids are. I've been looking for you."

They all stared up at him, fearfully, but nobody said anything.

"What've you been doing?"

The silence was deafening. At last Maria spoke, her lips trembling slightly.

"We've just b-b-been listening to the r-r-radio, Dad."

He eyed her critically and then glanced at the little radio on the ground in the center of the tight circle.

"How come you have to listen to it way out here?" he asked. "We've got radios all over the house."

Maria continued. "We–we were just listening, that's all."

At that moment Doug swallowed hard.

"As a matter of fact, Uncle Clarence, we were listening to a Christian radio program."

Maria's gaze met Phil's and they cringed, fearfully, but Clarence seemed not to be listening. He had already started for the house.

"Well, come on," he called over his shoulder. "Your mother has supper ready and she's getting mighty put out waiting for the five of you to come and eat it."

The triplets looked at one another questioningly. It didn't seem to be true, somehow. But Uncle Clarence hadn't said anything about their listening to the broadcast. God was taking care of them – making it possible for them to get the spiritual help and strength they needed in spite of the fact that they could not go to church.

As they walked back to the ranch house prayers of thanksgiving welled in their hearts.

THE
DANNY ORLIS
SERIES

The Danny Orlis series, by Bernard Palmer, delivers a blend of adventure, mystery, and suspense through various settings—from the Canadian wilderness to Guatemalan jungles. Danny Orlis, an adept out-doorsman, skilled athlete, and committed Christian, employs his quick thinking, calm bravery, and biblical solutions to confront everyday problems and hair-raising dangers. Early stories focus on Danny navigating school life, sports, and outdoor challenges, while in later books, Danny and his wife Kay provide wisdom and guidance to youngsters facing lifelike situations and challenges. Having sold over two million copies, this series has made Palmer a renowned author in Christian youth literature. Palmer is also the author of the Felicia Cartright series and various other series for Christian youth.

AVAILABLE FROM WWW.ANEKOPRESS.COM